Praise for *Sooner*

"The author creates a real sense of place and time through carefully selected period details."
—*School Library Journal*

"Calvert injects some gritty realism not always found in coming-of-age-on-the-prairie stories. . . . Fans will welcome the second installment of Tyler's tale, and they'll hope that Calvert follows his adventures."
—*The Bulletin of the Center for Children's Books*

Patricia Calvert

SOONER

Troll

This paperback edition published in 1999. Reprinted by arrangement with
Atheneum Books for Young Readers, an imprint of Simon & Schuster's
Children's Publishing Division.

Printed in the United States of America.

10 9 8 7 6 5 4 3 2 1

Library of Congress Cataloging-in-Publication Data

Calvert, Patricia
Sooner / Patricia Calvert.
p.   cm.
Sequel to: Bigger.
Summary: With the realization that his father may not return now that
the Civil War is over, thirteen-year-old Tyler finds himself the man of
their Missouri farm and the master of a new dog, the strikingly-colored
Sooner.
ISBN 0-8167-6322-4 (pbk.)
[1. Farm life—Missouri—Fiction. 2. Missouri—Fiction. 3. Dogs—Fiction.
4. Reconstruction—Fiction. 5. United States—History—1865–1898—
Fiction.] I. Title.
PZ7.C139So   1998
[Fic]—dc21
97-28007
CIP AC

For Bette Calvert,
with affection

Before . . .

On Sunday morning, April 9, 1865, General Robert E. Lee, leader of the Confederate forces during the Civil War, rose before the sun was up.

He dressed with special care in a fresh gray uniform, tied a scarlet sash around his waist, and mounted his favorite gray horse, Traveller. He made his way through the fog toward Appomattox Court House in Virginia. One of his aides preceded him, carrying a white towel tied to the end of a pole. When they reached their destination, Lee surrendered to General Ulysses S. Grant, commander of the Union forces. Thus ended the bloody four-year "War Between the States," in which more than half a million men lost their lives.

However, one of Lee's subordinates refused to concede defeat.

General Joseph O. Shelby—"Jo" to his men—commander of the Iron Brigade of Missouri, vowed he'd never surrender. Instead, he led his men to Texas. They crossed the Rio Grande at a place called Eagle Pass, then took refuge in Mexico. Shelby hoped to persuade Emperor Maximilian to supply him with fresh arms and horses. Appeals to the emperor were futile; his own luck had run out, and Maximilian was executed by Mexican revolutionaries in June 1867.

After President Andrew Johnson granted amnesty to all Civil War deserters, Shelby abandoned what he and his men called "a lost cause." The general returned to Bates County, Missouri, where he resumed the life of a farmer. He began to raise an important new crop—hemp—used to make rope, cordage, and canvas, which were in great demand as settlers moved west in large numbers when the war ended.

Nevertheless, a handful of Shelby's rebels never returned to their homes. They clung to dreams of a reborn Confederacy and drifted farther away to such places as Cuba, Venezuela, and Brazil. Gradually their names were lost to history. Their kinfolk often wondered what had become of their fathers, husbands, and brothers. At last, one family found out. . . .

Chapter One

SOMETIMES, AFTER TYLER BOHANNON WOKE EARLY, he lay as still as a fallen log beside his sleeping brother and let his mind gather itself to meet the new day. He watched the cool, blue Missouri dawn creep slowly through the high window under the eaves in the loft he shared with Lucas and his sister, Rosa Lee.

On such mornings, Tyler asked himself silently, *Am I really home again?* Or had he just waked from a dream, never having been gone from Sweet Creek at all? In those not-quite-awake moments, it wasn't easy to decide what was fact and what was fancy.

Perhaps he'd only imagined he'd once befriended a fierce, renegade black dog named Bigger, who died with a madman's bullet in his heart. . . .

Maybe he'd only dreamed there was a battlefield far away in Arkansas called Pea Ridge, where the bleached skulls of dead men bloomed like pale flowers in the mild green grass. . . .

He might never have met a boy named Isaac Peerce, who wore a red scar that flashed like a lightning bolt across his cheek to the corner of his mouth. . . .

As blue light filled the room, Tyler sifted through the memories that rose like trout coming to feed from the bottom of a deep pool. Most fanciful of all, maybe he'd only dreamed that he found Papa camped on the banks of the Rio Grande along with the rest of General Jo Shelby's ragtag army. Because how could Papa—after four long years of separation— turn away from him after they'd found each other again? What sort of man would do that to a son he claimed as his own?

Such a thing could happen only in a dream.

Tyler sat bolt upright on his corn-husk mattress and hugged his knees hard. He bent forward to rest his forehead against his knees. He flinched. There was a tender lump just beneath the skin.

Then it wasn't a dream! Months ago, when he'd gone in search of Papa, he'd been knocked unconscious by a rock hurled from Isaac Peerce's slingshot. Even after all this time, the knot was still painful. No, none of it was a dream.

In her narrow pine cot against the far wall—Rosa Lee was the only one who rated a regular bed—his sister sucked noisily on her fingers. Tyler smiled ruefully. Why, she was almost six years old!—way too big to still be doing such a baby thing as that.

He glanced down at his brother sleeping soundly beside him. The familiar sight of Lucas, his mouth open wide enough to catch flies, together with the steady slurp-slurp from Rosa Lee's cot a few feet away, anchored Tyler securely in the here and now.

"What matters now is I'm home again where I belong," Tyler whispered to himself. Back home and safe in the two-room cabin beside Sweet Creek. Yes, it was true Papa refused to come back—but he'd held himself to a different code.

Tyler sighed. It was the tug of ordinary life that pulled him away from the brink of desertion. Because wasn't it a mighty big temptation to cross the Rio Grande at Papa's side, never to look back, to head straight on down to Mexico with all the rest of Jo Shelby's followers?

You doggone well bet it was!

Instead, Tyler waited on the far side of the wide brown river, had hooked his arm around Bigger's thick neck. He'd held on hard to the black dog, as a drowning man holds on to the edge of a raft, and watched as Papa vanished on the far horizon.

Mama, Lucas, and Rosa Lee had already lost one of their men, he told himself. They didn't need to lose a second one. And now that he was home, he aimed to help Mama run the farm, raise up Lucas and Rosa Lee as best he could, make do as grown-up folks like Uncle Matt thought was his duty.

Tyler realized he ought to feel proud of himself. A little puffed up. Happy, even. After all, the war left plenty of folks—mostly those in the South—without roofs over their heads, without cows or chickens or crops.

General Sherman had vowed to scorch the earth of the Confederacy and he'd kept his word. He'd laid waste to the whole city of Atlanta, had burned the place nearly to the ground. And when the war was finally over, some men came home with their arms and legs shot off, their eyes blinded, or their hearts turned to stone, making them different than they'd ever been before.

Tyler frowned.

Just the same, it wasn't easy to be happy merely because he was home again himself with his own arms and legs intact, his two eyes as keen-sighted as they'd always been. Truth was, no matter how often Tyler went over everything in his mind, a hollow space remained right in the middle of his chest where his heart was supposed to be.

Tyler rubbed his breastbone slowly with the flat of his palm, as if a steady, circular motion would revive the battered organ inside. He whispered again the name that had lured him all the way down to Texas. The name that had left him standing alone at Eagle Pass on the banks of the Rio Grande, his arm wrapped around the neck of the menacing black dog named Bigger.

"Black Jack Bohannon." Tyler said it softly, so neither Lucas nor Rosa Lee would be disturbed. He said it again, slowly. "Black . . . Jack . . . Bohannon."

There was still magic in Papa's name, and for a moment saying it out loud filled up the emptiness he felt inside. It was a measure of the man himself, wasn't it, full of gypsy gaiety and wild, rebel courage. Tyler sighed again and hugged his knees tighter.

Except that wasn't how Papa seemed at the end. He wasn't cheerful; he wasn't like a gypsy at all.

In his mind's eye, Tyler saw his father plainly on the final morning they spent together in Texas. Black Jack's hard black eyes were red-rimmed with weariness. His jaw was set as if it had been carved from granite. His mouth was pulled so tight across his teeth that his lips were a cruel slash. The fire inside him didn't glow anymore; it smoldered.

"I can't quit now, Ty," Papa had said. "Not till things get put back the way they were before them Union boys turned 'em upside down for us."

As far as Papa was concerned, the Confederacy hadn't been whupped. Nossir! Papa believed the South was on the run only temporarily, that the war had merely been recessed for a spell. The final outcome was yet to be decided, and he intended to have a say in it.

"There's goin' to be a true day of reckoning with those boys in blue!" Papa vowed. Then, without a backward glance, he'd turned away and crossed the wide, shallow Rio Grande.

When Black Jack got to the other side, Tyler waited for his father to turn and wave good-bye, to hold his arm up against the flat, blue desert sky. But Papa never looked back. *No, not once.* Instead, he turned his face resolutely toward Mexico with the rest of Shelby's rebel army.

Tyler remembered how fiercely he'd held on to Bigger that morning. Then he and the black dog watched as the figures on the horizon steadily grew smaller, smaller, diminished to the size of ants, finally vanished altogether. The skyline was left bleak and empty. The only sound was the moaning of the wind through the dry grass, the only sight was a hawk wheeling high overhead.

As he relived those moments, Tyler's heart flopped weakly in his chest like a fish thrown up on a riverbank. He rubbed his breastbone again, slowly, slowly. *Come back, Papa!* he cried soundlessly, and rested his head against his knees. *Oh, come back . . . come back!*

Beside him, Lucas stirred. He yawned, stretched, then blinked sleepily. Tyler looked down. Lucas was eleven, two years younger than he was himself, and his eyes were as dark as Papa's, his smile just as sudden and lively as Black Jack's used to be. Lucas landed a light, playful punch on Tyler's arm.

"Hey, Ty. I'm real glad you're home," he said.

"Me, too," Tyler agreed.

"Know what else?"

"No, what?"

"I'm real glad you fetched that new pup back from

Uncle Matt's. Did Cousin Clayton help you pick that name for him or did you think it up?"

"Why, shoot, better believe I conjured it up myself! Cousin Clayton isn't real big on ideas, if you remember rightly."

"Sooner. It fits him just right, don't it, Ty? Seein' as how you said you'd have gone back to get him sooner if you'd known what a fine dog he'd turn out to be."

It was Tyler's turn to land a playful punch. "Let's you and me go down and see how the little mutt's doing, all right?"

By then, the dawn had turned from blue to gold. Tyler and Lucas dressed quickly beneath its yellow warmth so as not to waken Rosa Lee. Downstairs, Mama was already rattling the stove lids. In his sock feet, Lucas was the first to start down the steep, open stairs into the kitchen, giving Tyler a chance to admire from above how sleek and dark his brother's hair was. It fit his head as snug as a beaver cap.

Ah, so much like Papa's!

But Papa's not here, Tyler thought. I came back from Texas alone, and now there's Mama and Lucas and Rosa Lee to be looked after. And in spite of what Papa believed, the war *was* over. It was like Uncle Matt said: "A person can't keep looking over his shoulder, trying to make the past turn out different than it really did."

Beginning right now, there was a whole new life to be lived. Carrying his shoes, Tyler followed Lucas downstairs into the kitchen to meet another day.

Chapter Two

MAMA ALREADY HAD WASH WATER heating on the stove, and Sooner was still curled up fast asleep on a scrap of old saddle blanket next to the wood box. With his bushy cinnamon-colored tail folded neatly over his black nose, the new pup reminded Tyler of a fox he'd once seen dozing in the woods beyond Sweet Creek.

"I declare that critter hardly stays awake long enough to learn the sound of his own name," Mama teased with a smile. She hadn't yet wrapped her plain brown hair into a tight knot at the nape of her neck. It tumbled loosely onto her shoulders, making her seem not as careworn as usual.

"He's growing fast, Mama, and he needs plenty of sleep," Tyler said. He called the pup's name softly. "Sooner?" There was no response, not even the twitch of an ear.

"You there, *Soooo*-ner!" he called loudly. The pup struggled groggily to his feet and blinked against the morning light. He was Bigger's son, sure enough, and wore the same large white patch on his chest that his ferocious father had. As with Bigger, that patch was so snowy and perfectly shaped that Tyler was reminded again of a clean white bib a mother might tie around a baby's neck.

"No need to worry, Mama," Tyler said, laughing. "He knows his name all right." He reached down to give the pup a brisk good-morning rub behind the ears. Then he poured himself a basin of warm water, splashed some on his face, and scrubbed his hands with strong lye soap.

"Is Sooner much like that other dog you got when you went off to Texas to find Papa?" Lucas wanted to know.

Tyler studied the gangly pup as he dabbed his face and hands dry. Sooner yawned mightily, then stretched himself fore and aft to straighten the nighttime kinks out of his young bones. Even with his rear end cranked high in the air, his plumy, fox-colored tail began to wave the minute Lucas said his name.

"Well, Lucas," Tyler answered, "Bigger was a lot darker, about the shade of a burned-out pine log. You know, that funny charcoal color that's not exactly black, not gray either, just something dark in between? But his coat is like Bigger's—short and thick, like a bear cub's might be. Not to mention they both got those funny-colored eyes, as you can plainly see for yourself."

Lucas got down on his knees so he could peer directly into Sooner's eyes. He quickly got a free face washing from an eager pink tongue for his effort. "With one of 'em bein' blue like it is, and the other one brown, it's almost like there's two different dogs inside him," Lucas said.

It was a matter Tyler had often speculated about himself. Uncle Matt claimed those eyes were inherited from an ancestor that came from the Highlands of Scotland. He explained that sheepdogs from that part of the world often had one eye of brown, the other of blue. But in Bigger's case, it wasn't merely having eyes of two different colors that made it impossible for him to be an ordinary dog.

"On account of the way Bigger'd been treated, I doubt he was ever goin' to be a family dog," Tyler went on, remembering how Bigger had snarled and snapped the first time he tried to pet him. "What I mean is, he was never goin' to be a dog all of us could share. Bigger'd been ruined for that. He was all business—mean business, that is."

"Tell me again what that man did to Bigger to make him so ornery," Lucas urged, taking his turn at the washbasin while Mama stirred up a pot of cornmeal mush.

Tyler shrugged agreeably. In the weeks since he'd come home, he'd told the same story dozens of times, had described the color of Bigger's coat and his eyes just as often, yet Lucas never seemed to tire of hearing it all again. Rosa Lee, who came straggling down from the loft, sleep marks printed like scars on her cheeks, called loudly that she wanted to hear, too.

"That fella who owned Bigger first—I never did find out his name—why, he told me how he used to torment Bigger just to make him crazy-mean. Said he wanted to make him so wicked he'd have a temper hotter than a banked fire. That way, he'd be a better guard dog. Kept Bigger tied up all the time. Didn't feed him regular. Poked him with sharp sticks. Shoot! With that kind of treatment, a person could make a mean dog outta the best pooch in the world."

It pained Tyler to realize he probably didn't know everything about Bigger's past. No doubt other evil deeds had been committed against him to guarantee he'd be so dangerous only a fool would go near him.

Each time he heard the story, Lucas got more indignant. Now he whacked the flat of his wet hand so hard against the tabletop that Sooner yipped and scuttled behind Tyler's knees.

"Know what I'd a done to that man?" Lucas seethed, his black eyes narrowed with revenge, his teeth clenched. "Why, I might've took up a rock or a big stick with a knot on the end of it and I might've hauled off and . . . and killed that man!"

"Whoa there, Lucas," Tyler soothed. "Don't come to such a quick boil. No need to talk so easy about killing anyone." For a split second, Lucas's wrath reminded Tyler so much of Papa's rage against the North that it nearly took his breath away.

Well, it *was* true that Lucas seemed to be much more Papa's son than he was himself. It was a realization that always made Tyler feel a trifle melancholy. It was his own fate to have ended up being exactly like Mama's storekeeper brother, Uncle Matt: quiet, steady, accountable. Lucas and Papa, on the other hand, had the same fierce indignation lurking right below the surface, the same passion to see wrongs set to right.

"Anyway, I'm pretty sure the folks over in McMinnville who saw that fella shoot Bigger made sure he paid his dues," Tyler added, hoping Lucas would be placated. That day was still painfully fresh in his own mind. The way that man reached for his pistol . . . how he knelt on one knee to fire . . . the echo of two shots . . . the second one causing a scarlet stain to bloom like a rose on Bigger's clean white bib.

"But if he hadn't killed Bigger, then you wouldn't have had to get you another dog!" Rosa Lee exclaimed, her curls a dark halo around her face. Like Lucas, she, too, had Papa's midnight-colored hair and his flashing black eyes. Alas, his own hair was brown and straight, his eyes a common blue like Uncle Matt's.

"Well, I did. *We* did," Tyler corrected himself. "If I'd brought Bigger back to Sweet Creek, though, he would only have been my dog, not anybody else's. That's just the way he was. But Sooner here—well, he's only a pup, and we can start him out right. He'll end up being a friend to each of us, yet a good watchdog, too. We can teach him proper manners if we always treat him right."

"Don't want to change the subject on you," Mama said as she dished the cornmeal into four bowls, "but this being Saturday with no school and all, it would be a good day for you boys to go over to the Snepps' place to see about getting us a mule." She'd been talking about a mule ever since he got home from Texas, but for the life of him, Tyler couldn't imagine where the money would come from to make such a purchase.

"If we aim to put that hillside in corn again—a bigger crop next year than last, so we can maybe have a little extra to sell—then you boys are goin' to need more muscle power than just your own two backs," she declared, and set a pitcher of sorghum on the table.

"How much you figure we got to spend?" Tyler asked, lacing his mush with the glossy brown syrup. He glanced out the window above the empty chair where Papa used to sit. Mama was surely right about the day; it was one of those blue-and-gold autumn kind that made a person glad just to be alive. Such a day was almost enough to convince a person he could eventually be happy again. Even without Papa.

"Well now, that's a problem all right," Mama admitted. She sighed and pushed a lock of brown hair from her cheek. "All I've got scraped together is three dollars. Four, at the most. Except I'd been hoping to hang on to that other dollar to put aside for Christmas."

"I surely don't know what kind of a mule we can get for three dollars," Tyler grumbled, spooning mush into his mouth. Oh, how he hated to think of going over to the Snepps' with such a miserable, pitiful sum! It would be as if he and Lucas had come begging. Asking for charity. Throwing themselves on the mercy of neighbors who were better off. He'd just as soon die as do such a thing.

Tyler could just imagine the look in Oat Snepp's pale eyes, that down-his-nose expression he always wore in Mr. Blackburn's class at Two Mile school. As if he came from folks that were better than the rest of the world could ever hope to be. (He'd have to temper that look just a little if Papa had come home, though, wouldn't he?)

"Might be you could make some kind of agreement with Oat's daddy," Mama went on, as if she understood he was thinking of Oat's uppityness. "Elway Snepp has always been a decent fellow, and he knows what it's like to lose someone in the war. He lost his oldest boy, Billy, at Stones River, remember? He'll want to do what's fair, especially since he knows we Bohannons are on our own now."

On our own now. Those four words kindled a blaze of resentment in Tyler's breast. "Don't say that, Mama!" he exclaimed. "Don't talk like it's a forever thing!" Under the table, Sooner, who had been nestled snugly between Tyler's sock feet, flinched at the hard sounds that crossed the table above.

"Papa might come home; he just might!" Sooner shuddered again, so Tyler lowered his voice. "You can't tell but what he'll come riding across the bridge any day now," he said through gritted teeth, "then we'll be a regular family again. He'll step through that door, and things'll be the same as they always were."

Mama gathered up the empty blue mush bowls from the table. Her lowered gaze hid what she was thinking, but there was a firm set to her mouth, and Tyler was pretty sure he knew exactly what was in her mind. *I know your papa, son,* she was thinking. *He won't be back. Not today. Not tomorrow. Not ever.*

"It might take him awhile, but I know he'll come home," Tyler insisted, even though she hadn't said a word out loud.

"Well, meantime, you boys go on over to see Elway Snepp, hear?" This time, the tone in her voice left no room for argument. "I'll pack you up a lunch so you won't have to take a meal at their table. We're not that poor, not yet." Then she held four dollars out to Tyler. Tyler looked at them and laid one back in her palm.

"Hang on to it for Christmas," he muttered, surprised how puny and mewling his voice sounded in his own ears. Any fool knew that even the sorriest kind of mule would cost at least twenty dollars. If a family wanted a real good animal, why, they'd have to pay forty for sure. For three, you were likely to get something moth-eaten and spavined, partly blind, its back slung low as a hammock stretched between two trees. A three-dollar mule would have all the work worked out of it long ago.

"We'll take whatever we can get," Tyler told her. "If we end up having to spend more, well, maybe I can do day work for Mr. Snepp when harvesttime comes till we get the critter paid off." The thought of hiring out, giving Oat a chance to breathe down his neck or watch from his daddy's front porch, stuck in Tyler's craw.

"Lordy, goin' over to the Snepps' will be fun, Ty," Lucas said, oblivious of the storm of protest in Tyler's heart. "As we walk along, you can tell me again about all those folks you met when you went lookin' for Papa.

Like that old lady who told you about them pesky scalawags and how they steal things from folks."

"I want to go, too! You ain't the only one who wants to hear about scalawags!" Rosa Lee yelped, her lower lip stuck out far enough for a bird to perch on it. Tyler could plainly see she was getting set to raise a fit.

"It's a fair piece over to the Snepps', and it'll take us most of the day to get there and back," he warned, hoping she'd be reasonable. "You're too little. Maybe some other—"

"Oh, goodness, let her tag along," Mama interrupted gently. "If you get a mule like I hope you do, Rosa Lee can ride all the way home. It'll be a good way for the three of you to spend time together."

Tyler knew he'd been outmaneuvered, and he tucked the money in his pocket. Maybe part of growing up was doing things you hated to do. Because it sure caused a storm of misery inside him to go begging from the Snepps. With three dollars to buy a mule, that's the only thing it could be called. Plain flat-out begging.

Tyler squared his shoulders. He decided to make light of his true feelings. Under the table, he gave the new pup a playful nudge with his big toe. "Well, if Rosa Lee gets to come along, we'll let Sooner go, too. He can chase rabbits all the way over to the Snepps' and all the way back."

Sooner scooted out from under the table as if he understood every word. He waved his plumy red tail merrily as if it were a flag on a pole, his brown eye as gleeful as any ordinary pup's. The blue one was distant and thoughtful, as if he were recalling ancient tales passed on to him by those forebears in the Highlands.

Chapter Three

THE MORNING SUN warmed the backs of their necks as they walked along, and the lunch Tyler carried wrapped in a clean cloth was a pleasant weight as it dangled from his right fist. Sooner spied a rabbit on the far side of Sweet Creek and went sifting across the bridge in hot pursuit. For a moment, Tyler forgot there were only three dollars in his pocket.

"Lucas wanted you to tell us more stories, so tell some," Rosa Lee demanded as their footsteps echoed across the bridge. She'd gotten fond of those yarns, too, Tyler mused, even if there were a lot of things she wasn't old enough yet to understand.

Even if she had been, there were things Tyler knew he couldn't tell her or Lucas. Not Mama, either. About that cemetery at Pea Ridge, for instance. He didn't know himself what he thought about all those bleached bones laid out on the grass in a half-orderly fashion. The tatters of Northern blue and Confederate gray uniforms had been all mixed together. . . . There was a pile of belt buckles, eyeglasses, and shoes the dead men had worn. . . . In a smaller separate pile were notebooks and letters and pictures the soldiers had carried from home. Was it seemly that such pitiful things were the sum of men's lives?

Tyler recalled what the grave digger said that afternoon: "Dead, all men look alike. These chaps are brothers now, whether they aimed to be in life or not." The old man looked troubled as he spoke, as if he were asking himself what the war had been about. Tyler swung the lunch at his side and hummed tunelessly to remind himself that he wasn't at Pea Ridge now. He was on his way to the Snepps' to buy a mule.

"Tell us again about that boy named Isaac," Lucas urged, having forgotten he'd wanted to hear about the old woman who talked about scalawags. The request pulled Tyler's thoughts even farther away from the battlefield in Arkansas, with its burden of frail white bones laid out on the green grass.

"Umm, Isaac," Tyler murmured. He liked to think about Isaac himself; telling stories about him would be an easy task. "Well, what you noticed about Isaac right off was he was a black boy," he began. "Made him different from us. I mean, he couldn't live like you and me, not being a free person and all. The whole war was fought over folks like Isaac, about whether or not it was right to buy and sell people like him, about whether you could trade 'em away from their families without asking their opinion in the matter."

"Buy? You mean like we are goin' to buy us a mule today from Mr. Snepp?" Rosa Lee wanted to know. It was hard for her to keep up, so Tyler slowed his pace a bit. Anyway, it was easier to tell stories if a person wasn't concentrating on hiking so lively down the road.

"Just like that," Tyler told her. "Doesn't seem right, does it, buying a person same's you'd buy a mule?" Rosa Lee frowned and shook her head. "In fact, Isaac's daddy got sold away while Isaac was still a baby in his mama's belly," Tyler added. "Hadn't even been born yet! Means Isaac never got to know his own father."

Months had passed since Isaac told that story, yet such a fate still astonished Tyler. "Imagine—never having a chance to know your own papa!" he exclaimed. Even with his faults (sometimes Papa came home from McMinnville smelling sweetly of whiskey, having forgotten to bring back the flour and sugar Mama wanted), Tyler couldn't imagine never knowing him at all.

"Hold on, Ty. That business about owning a black person—" Lucas put in quickly, and Tyler noticed there was a belligerent note in his brother's voice—"that's what Papa believed! That's why he rode off with Jo Shelby's men in the first place," Lucas said. "That means buying and selling black folks can't be all wrong, or Papa wouldn't have gone along with it."

Tyler wanted to make sure both Lucas and Rosa Lee understood what Papa *really* believed, because the oftener he thought about Isaac the more important it seemed to be.

"Me and Papa talked about that, Lucas," he explained. "Papa said it wasn't that he wanted to put anybody in chains. You know as well as me that *he* never owned a slave. Not like Uncle Matt, down in New Hope, who owned Henry. Our papa never put chains on anyone! But he sure hated for those folks in the North to tell the rest of us what we could or couldn't do. You know Papa—being told what to do didn't set well with him, no matter who did the telling."

Lucas stopped dead in the middle of the road. Tyler walked on with Rosa Lee, figuring his brother needed to pick a rock out of his shoe or make water in the weeds along the ditch. The high-pitched, anguished wail that

Lucas suddenly let out made Tyler drop his towel-wrapped parcel. He whirled, his heart hammering with alarm.

"Lucas! Lordy, boy, what happened? A snake bite you? You got a bad pain somewhere?"

"Why didn't you take me to Texas with you?" Lucas cried. "Oh, Ty, why didn't you?"

Tyler was struck dumb by the grief in his brother's voice, not to mention how Lucas's eyes were squinched shut with pain and his mouth was a round, open *O* of utter misery. "If I'd gone with you, Ty, Icould've seenPapaonemoretime!" Some of Lucas's words were hard to understand because they were mooshed together in a long wail of despair. "It ain't fair you're theonly oneinthefamilywhodid!"

Tears ran down Lucas's cheeks, and seeing him cry made Rosa Lee turn down her mouth and start to whimper, too. Tyler stepped forward quickly and grabbed Lucas around the shoulders. He pulled his brother close and hugged him hard. *Lordy, lordy!* He knew exactly what that terrible, gnawing pain felt like. It was the same agony he'd felt himself as he'd watched Papa mount up and head for Mexico, never once looking back, never once offering a farewell wave.

"IlovedPapajustasmuchasyoudid, Ty," Lucas mumbled damply against Tyler's shoulder. "He was my daddy, too. So it ain't fair—it just ain't fair—" His words soon drowned in the wetness of his snuffles.

"Easy, Lucas," Tyler soothed. He patted his brother on the back the way he'd seen ladies burp babies. Only Lucas wasn't a baby, and Tyler was surprised to note how tall his brother was getting, how square and lean his shoulders were.

Who'd have thought he'd already come almost up to

my collarbone? Tyler marveled. Lucas was shooting up just like the stalk in that story Mama used to read about a boy who traded a cow for a bunch of beans, then climbed up to the sky to outwit a giant and came home with a pocketful of gold.

Baby or not, Lucas hung on like one, and the sounds he made were rusty, as if he hadn't had much practice crying. Tyler felt Rosa Lee pluck at his trouser leg, so he dropped an arm and pulled her against his hip. Over the top of Lucas's head he could see Sooner up near the three bare apple trees where he'd buried Bigger so many weeks ago. Oh, my! There was grief enough in life to go around, wasn't there?

Even though they'd hardly gotten a good start on their trip to the Snepps', they stood awhile in the middle of the sunny road and clung to each other. Sometimes, Tyler decided, that was the only thing folks could do. Just hang on tight to each other, and hope the misery got easier to carry.

Elway Snepp had just left his handsome red barn and was heading up to his house when Tyler hailed him down. For a moment, Tyler was afraid he might not remember who he and Lucas and Rosa Lee were. As they approached, he saw Mr. Snepp study them narrowly from beneath his hat brim, his expression suspicious. When they got closer, his frown finally changed to a cautious half-smile of surprise.

"Why, it's the Bohannon chil'ren, ain't it?" he asked. "Yes, it most surely is," he said, answering his own question. "If you young ones have come all the way from your place down there on Sweet Creek, I'd say you've done a goodly bit of traveling this mornin'."

Elway Snepp had a wide, freckled face—plain, like Uncle Matt's—neither homely nor handsome, neither thin nor fat, just something common in between. In the looks department, neither man could hold a candle to Papa.

Mr. Snepp glanced down at Sooner. "Got yourselves a new pup, too, I see." He looked a little more closely. "Why, ain't he a funny-lookin' critter, having one blue eye like that and one brown one? Don't know I'd trust a dog with eyes such as them."

"Oh, he's a fine dog," Tyler said quickly. "Got a mighty easy disposition. Uncle Matt says those weird eyes come from his ancestors in the Highlands of Scotland." Sooner looked up at Mr. Snepp, his red tongue lolling out the side of his mouth, and wagged his back end agreeably as if to demonstrate he was an honorable pooch.

Mr. Snepp hooked his thumbs in his suspenders. "Well, now. What brings you this way all by yourselves, chil'ren?"

"I'm Tyler, the oldest, Mr. Snepp," Tyler said, not wanting to be lumped in a pile as one of "the chil'ren," which would make it hard to talk business man to man. He held out his hand, not surprised that Mr. Snepp's handshake was limp, not a knuckle buster, like Papa's.

"This is Lucas, and this here is our baby sister, Rosa Lee. We come over today to do some bargaining. That is, if you got time to talk business with us."

"Bargaining, you say?" Mr. Snepp echoed, his careful half-smile shrinking a bit. Tyler noticed that his freckled cheeks were rather full, giving him a chipmunky look. "Well, then, you come on up to the house. I was just goin' in for dinner myself, and you young ones are welcome to have a bite, too."

"Nossir, we don't need to do that," Tyler said, and

patted the lunch he carried. "Our mama fixed us up fine. If you're willing, why don't we just do our business right here?" Tyler hoped doing so would make it unlikely they'd run into Oat. After losing his older brother in the war, Oat was more eager than ever to be front and center. In Mr. Blackburn's class down at Two Mile school, he always had his hand up, grabbing at the air as if it held invisible rungs on a ladder, wanting to be first to climb to the top with the answer to everything.

"Well then, let's us just sit down over there in the shade of the barn," Mr. Snepp said. "We can settle ourselves on that old sawbuck, and you chil'ren can tell me what's on your minds."

Sooner flopped on the ground, glad for a chance to rest. As soon as Mr. Snepp was seated, Tyler got down to business without further trifling small talk.

"My mama wants to put that whole slope behind our house—it's land that drains well and faces south—into corn next spring, and we need ourselves a mule, Mr. Snepp. With me and Lucas doing all the work now, it'll be just too big a job for the two of us with only a spade and hoe between us."

"A mule, eh?" Mr. Snepp nodded his head in the direction of a nearby pen. "Well, I got me a team over there, but I couldn't let one of that pair go." They were big, dark, handsome beasts with tall, alert ears, their gleaming haunches as ripply with muscle as washboards.

"I got so much farmwork to do myself I'm afraid I couldn't even loan one of 'em out, much less sell one. Truth is, son, I don't think I can help you much."

How quickly a business deal could be handled when there was no business to do, Tyler thought with an inward sigh. Mr. Snepp lifted his hat, wiped his forehead with the back of his hand, then resettled the hat over his thin red hair. He squinted hard at each of them, which made Rosa Lee turn pink and start to wiggle her feet in the dust.

"Tell you what," Mr. Snepp went on, "there's a near-worthless, broke-down old mule I got in a pasture by the pond in back of the barn. Don't know why I didn't shoot the critter a long while ago. He likes to eat, sure enough, but can't do much to earn his keep anymore. Guess I worked him nearly to death during the years when I could afford only a single mule instead of a good team."

"How old is he?" Tyler asked warily. "How broke down?"

"Gracious, the old boy must be at least eighteen, twenty by now," Mr. Snepp admitted. "Shows his age considerable, too."

"That's old, all right," Tyler agreed.

Elway Snepp studied each of them again. "Now, I don't aim to be nosy, chil'ren, but didn't somebody tell me your daddy never came back from the war? And are you tellin' me now that you boys and your mama aim to do all the field work by yourselves?"

It was the type of question that made Tyler feel as squirmy as Rosa Lee. For something to do, he poked at Sooner's side with his toe. The pup was so worn out he only gave a tired grunt.

"Well, sir, it's true my daddy went off with General Shelby, who don't believe the war is really over," he admitted. "But Papa'll be back eventually—meantime, me and Lucas got to look after ourselves and our mama."

"Better look after me, too!" Rosa Lee exclaimed, indignant that she didn't hear her name mentioned.

"Now, about that old mule—"

For a moment, Elway Snepp was silent. "Well, life is hard on all of us, ain't it, chil'ren? Seems like the good

Lord gives us burdens we never counted on carrying."
He dabbed at his brow again, and Tyler noticed he
seemed about to hold a long private conversation with
himself.

"About that old mule," Tyler prompted a second
time.

"Like I said, he's down there in a little pasture behind
the barn." Mr. Snepp jerked a thumb over his shoulder.
"You go on down there and take a look at him. Old fella's
seen better days, but if you're desperate enough, he might
be what you're lookin' for. Then you come on up to the
house and maybe we can figure out what he might be
worth." He said *old fella* as if it were actually the animal's
name.

Old Fella stood alone with his head lowered and his
eyes closed. He didn't seek the shade, and Tyler figured
it was because his bones were so cold and brittle the
autumn sun felt mighty good as it warmed him. The
hairs on the mule's muzzle were silver; his ears were
rimmed with frost; his lashes were tipped with white. He
didn't seem to notice their approach. He didn't budge
even when they walked up to stand three feet from him.

"He looks sad," Rosa Lee said mournfully.

She sure was right about that, Tyler thought. Old, sad,
and all used up. How could such an animal be expected to
pull a plow along that hillside in back of the house, which
in some spots was pretty steep? This critter looked so
poorly Tyler realized he might have to tell Mama she'd
better give up her idea about having a bigger corn harvest
next year.

"Hey, Old Fella," Lucas said, and didn't try to hide
his disappointment. The mule's silvery lashes flickered,

then he studied each of them with weary patience. He shifted his weight from one side to the other and wasn't alarmed when Sooner sniffed at each of his four feet all the way up to the knee. Tyler laid his hand carefully on two large pale patches on the mule's withers. Long ago, a poorly fitting harness must have worn his hide off, and the hair had grown back white.

"He's way past his prime," Lucas groaned. "Looks like he'd drop dead on us before we got him halfway home."

"But he's good sized," Tyler pointed out, trying to look on the bright side of the situation. And he was, nearly sixteen hands tall. "Between now and planting time maybe we can figure out a way to put him in shape."

"No way we can shave years off his age, which is his main problem," Lucas muttered.

"We could feed him good," Tyler insisted. "You and Rosa Lee could scour that cornfield for what didn't get picked up this year. We could rub him down with liniment every day to get his circulation going. There might be a couple years' worth of work left in his old carcass. Anyway, with only three dollars to spend, I don't see we've got much choice."

They stood in silence, inspecting the mule, who shut his eyes and seemed to doze off again. "Should we vote on it?" Tyler suggested.

"Vote! Vote!" Rosa Lee cried gleefully, and jumped around the pen as if she'd been invited to play an exciting new game. Even when Sooner started to bark, the racket scarcely roused the mule from his stupor. Then Rosa Lee suddenly was struck by doubt.

"What's that mean, *vote?* How do we do it, Ty?"

"When I ask a question, you and Lucas just holler out yes or no. Now, everybody ready?"

"Ready!" Lucas and Rosa Lee yelled in unison.

"Should we try to buy this old broke-down mule for three dollars?"

"Yes!" they both cried, and Sooner yipped his agreement.

"All right, let's go see what sort of a deal we can strike with Mr. Snepp," Tyler declared. Going up to the house meant they'd most likely come nose to nose and toes to toes with Oat, but there was no way to get out of it now.

Tyler gave his thigh a smart slap to bring Sooner to heel, then strode toward the Snepps' wide, white front porch. Lucas and Rosa Lee ran alongside, giddy with the prospect of stepping inside someone else's house. Even Tyler felt a vague thrill to think he might be able to take a mule home to Mama after all.

Chapter Four

THE SNEPP HOME WASN'T AS WELL-KEPT-UP as Tyler expected it would be, given the grand impression it made from outside.

Mama was fussy about *her* kitchen and kept it as tidy as possible. The floor was swept twice a day and the tabletop and stove were always brushed clean. Dishes were stacked neatly on plain pine shelves with a piece of flour-sack curtain drawn across the front to keep plates, bowls, and cups free of dust. By comparison, the Snepps' kitchen looked as if the lady of the house hadn't tended to it in a good long while, or else she was the careless kind.

Yet there were stew bowls on the table, and the Snepp children—all of them were boys, Tyler noticed, including a pair of redheaded twins younger than Rosa Lee—were feeding their faces and squabbling among themselves as noisily as geese. And lo and behold, refilling each bowl with a ladle, a soiled dish towel tied around his waist as if he'd been cooking all morning, was none other than uppity Oat Snepp!

Tyler didn't know who was more astonished, Oat or

himself. With that towel around his middle, Oat sure didn't look very superior. He flashed an indignant glance in his father's direction as if to say, *You should've warned me there was going to be company for dinner, Pa!*

"Oat has been doing the cooking since his mama got sick," Mr. Snepp explained, paying no mind to Oat's glare. "He don't do too bad, either. The missus tells him how to manage, and danged if he don't follow orders real good. Now, Oat, whyn't you set out three more bowls for the Bohannon chil'ren?"

Tyler wanted to protest but kept his mouth shut. Sometimes a person could make things worse by trying to make them better. In a fluster, Oat filled three new bowls, then replenished a cracked plate in the middle of the table with hunks of bread he sawed off a fresh loaf.

Tyler was embarrassed to see how greedily Lucas and Rosa Lee attacked their meal. A person would think they hadn't been fed in a week. He hoped Mr. Snepp hadn't noticed, and to distract the farmer's attention, he steered the conversation toward the subject of deal making.

"You're right about that mule being old, Mr. Snepp," he began, clearing his throat and trying to sound as if he were an old hand at doing business. "So I was wondering—him being so long in years and so poorly—what you think he might be worth."

"Let me turn that around," Elway Snepp countered. "What d'you think Old Fella might be worth to *you?*"

Tyler hesitated. He hated to think how little he had to spend. Only the fact that Oat was standing over there next to the stove with a towel around his middle, rattling the grate and fussing with the stew kettle like an old housewife, made the job easier.

"My mama sent three dollars with me, which I grant you ain't much even for such a poor critter." Tyler heard

Oat give a loud snort when he mentioned the sum. He'd be quick to blab it all over Two Mile school, too. "I told Mama I'd hire out to you to work off whatever else might be owed, though, so you just name your price."

Mr. Snepp finished his stew thoughtfully, then mopped the bowl with a piece of bread. Tyler could see Oat grind his teeth. He doesn't want me to come back here to work off a debt any more'n I want to, he realized.

"You're right about three dollars not bein' much, but Old Fella isn't, either," Elway Snepp admitted. "So you can take him for the amount you've mentioned, and I hope he lives long enough to do you a little bit of good. If it turns out he dies on you right quick, why, I'll be glad to give you back half the selling price."

As Tyler fished in his pocket for the money, a faint cry came from a room at the back of the house. "Your mother is calling," Mr. Snepp said quietly to Oat. "You'd best go see what she needs, son."

"Huh! Three dollars for a mule!" Oat guffawed as he flew out of the kitchen. This time there was no doubt about his opinion.

Mr. Snepp leaned his arms on the table and murmured in a tired, flat voice, "We had us another baby awhile back. It was a girl, which me and Mrs. Snepp wanted mighty bad, seeing we'd never had one." He smiled faintly at Rosa Lee as he spoke.

"But our daughter was a poor, blue little mite right from her first breath and didn't live through her first day on this earth. Lottie never seemed to get well after that, and with Billy gone and no female in the house to cook and clean and look after the other young ones, Oat was the only one to take over."

Mr. Snepp fixed Tyler with a level gaze. "In this house, we know what it is to have hard times, just like you folks do down there on Sweet Creek." He held Tyler's glance so long that Tyler began to fidget in his chair.

"Now, you say you folks are fixing to put that whole long hillside at your place into corn?" Mr. Snepp went on, rousing himself out of his own troubles. When Papa was home, Elway Snepp had stopped by now and then, so Tyler knew he understood exactly the spot Mama had in mind.

"Yessir, that's what my mama wants to do," Tyler said.

"Well, the coming crop in these parts is hemp. Hemp—for making rope, you know. You tell your mama there's a fine market for it, what with Abe Lincoln signing that Homestead Act back in 1862 before that fella—wasn't his name Booth?—shot him dead. Why, ev'rybody heading west now that the war's over will need cordage and canvas and such like—farmers and river men and cattlemen alike. Yessir, take my word for it— hemp is the coming crop and will bring smart farmers a fine price."

Hemp. Tyler frowned. He had no idea what it looked like, how it grew, or when it was harvested. "I'll sure tell my mama about that," he promised nevertheless. Covertly, when Mr. Snepp wasn't looking, he sneaked a hunk of bread for Sooner, who was waiting patiently on the porch outside.

It wouldn't be polite to say so, but Tyler doubted Mama would be one whit interested in Mr. Snepp's idea. After all, they already knew how to raise corn and even had plenty of seed for next year. A family could do so many things with corn: eat it fresh, grind it into meal, soak it in lye to make hominy, feed it to chickens, fatten a pig with it, feed it to a milk cow, sell it if there was any left over. Not to mention folks might be able to put an old mule in shape by feeding him corn. Corn was a sure

thing. Hemp? Well, let well-off farmers like Elway
Snepp take their chances on it.

It wasn't easy to get Old Fella to follow. It was as if
he'd been standing so long in one place he'd rather not be
bothered changing his address. But after a few tottery
steps and blinking dazedly in the afternoon sunlight,
they finally got him pointed in the right direction and
headed down the road. Tyler waited until they were out
of sight of the Snepp place before he asked Rosa Lee if
she wanted to ride.

Five travelers now instead of four, they all walked
silently as shadows lengthened in the road. Going home,
Sooner didn't chase any more rabbits; he was tired, too,
not having had as many naps as he was used to. Lucas
and Rosa Lee didn't ask to hear any more stories; even if
they had, Tyler didn't feel like telling any. It was as if
they'd all worn themselves out with visiting and doing
business, and it was a pleasure to travel wordlessly along.

When they got home, Mama regarded Old Fella with
a skeptical eye. "Goodness' sakes, he isn't much, is he?"
she lamented, and cupped her chin in her palm.

"Mr. Snepp said he'd give us half our money back if
the critter dies on us real quick," Lucas assured her.

"The old boy will be all right," Tyler insisted. "We
got till spring to put him in shape. When it gets cold, we
can feed him hot mash, like Papa used to feed Ransom."

The mention of Ransom made Lucas whirl about, his
dark eyes blazing. "Say, Ty—you never told us what happened to Ransom!"

Tyler wished he could tie a knot in his tongue. What
possessed him to mention Papa's tall, high-headed red
saddle horse? When Papa first brought him home as a

yearling, he'd bragged the colt was worth a king's ransom and ever after just called him Ransom. Whenever he used Ransom behind the plow, he always made sure there were no rough spots on the inside of the harness, so as not to damage his glossy red coat.

"I guess he got killed in the war," Tyler muttered. He remembered the day the two of them left Sweet Creek to go off to war; Ransom acted as eager for battle as Papa himself. "Mind you, I never found out for sure," Tyler added, "but that's what I figured must've happened. Why else would Papa be riding that ugly gray horse the last time I saw him?"

The whole conversation was taking a terrible turn and was bound to remind Lucas once again of the adventure he'd missed by not going to Texas. But there was no way both he and Lucas could have gone off and left Mama and Rosa Lee alone, Tyler wanted to explain. Someday, maybe he could.

"Well, let's get ourselves in to supper," Mama said with a heavy sigh. "In the clear light of day maybe this poor old has-been will look more like a might-be. Right now, boys, I confess he doesn't look like much to me." It was plain she figured they'd made a sorry bargain for the three dollars she'd worked so hard to save, but the simple truth was the choice had been Old Fella or no mule at all.

"I'll get him settled in a stall in the cow shed," Tyler said. "You all run up to the house and I'll be along in a minute." As the three of them turned to leave, Tyler waited to see what Sooner would do. Would he go with the others, knowing he'd get some supper, too? Or would he stay behind to be company? He was pleased when Sooner followed him into the cow shed and paid careful attention as the old mule was bedded down for the night.

Tyler ran his hands slowly over the mule's withers, back, rump. "The muscles under this old man's hide are stiff and hard as iron," he admitted. "Not ripply and elastic at all, like the muscles of that handsome pair in the Snepps' yard." Yet laying hands on the old chap, trying to assess his potential, gave Tyler a feeling of ownership.

"Good boy," he whispered. "You're goin' to be all right, ain't you?" He fetched some hay, which Old Fella picked at, blinked wearily, then fell into a doze before he could work up enough energy to eat.

"Tomorrow I'll send Lucas and Rosa Lee up to the field to get you some corn," Tyler promised. "Then we'll start to loosen you up. I'll set Lucas to walking you up and down the road a couple times a day. Afterward one of us will rub you down with some of Papa's old horse liniment. What we got to do, old man, is get your blood circulating again. Got to give you something to do besides wait around to die."

After tending Calico and her half-grown heifer calf, Tyler left the shed and shut the door behind him. Sooner danced around his knees, begging for permission to run toward the house. "Just hang on a minute," Tyler whispered.

This was the time of day he loved the best. The south hillside, where last year's corn crop was a picked-over field of stubble, was turning pink in the setting sun. From the house came the sounds of supper being put on the table. Sooner whined, as if to say, *Hurry, hurry!*

"A three-dollar mule won't ever amount to much," Tyler sighed, "but I'll wager you a bowl of table scraps he's goin' to work out just fine." Sooner wagged his plumy tail, signaling that he'd been patient long enough.

"Git along then, if you're so doggone hungry," Tyler teased. Sooner flew through the golden evening, and as the sun dropped lower, the stubble-covered hillside darkened.

Hemp, Mr. Snepp said. Claimed there was a good market for it because the West was opening up, that everyone headed out that way would need rope and canvas.

Tyler followed Sooner up the path. Maybe he'd talk to Mama about the new crop the first chance he got.

Chapter Five

TYLER HEARD LUCAS GET UP before there was any light in the loft. From the far side of the room came the familiar slurp-slurp from Rosa Lee's cot, then a furtive rustle of clothes as Lucas pulled on his trousers and shirt. Soft footfalls followed as his brother tiptoed to the steep stairs and descended quickly into the kitchen.

Tyler strained to hear what was going on below. He heard Lucas rouse Sooner from his bed beside the wood box, then listened to the snick of the pup's toenails on the bare wood floor. Next came a creak of hinges as Lucas opened the door, then let it close behind him. Tyler groaned. He pulled his quilt up to his chin and tried to go back to sleep. It was no use. He rolled off the pallet and fumbled in the dark for his own clothes.

Outside, the sky was still black, pocked with cold unfriendly stars, and a waning moon hung low on the horizon. Tyler hugged himself and shivered in the chill air. Papa—wherever he was down there in Mexico—was he looking up at the very same moon? Tyler hoped so and prayed that he was thinking of home.

Lucas had carried a lantern down to the cow shed

with him, and Tyler found him studying the old mule anxiously in its smoky glow. Nearby, Sooner sat respectfully on his haunches, ears upright, his strange eyes missing nothing. He regarded the new family member with as much concern as Lucas did.

"Did you think he was goin' to pass on to the Great Beyond during the night?" Tyler teased.

"Not exactly," Lucas answered huffily, "but I figured in case he did we'd better not waste any time hiking right over to Mr. Snepp's to get half our money back like he promised we could."

Tyler leaned his weight experimentally against the mule's side and was pleased when the animal braced himself and leaned right back. "I suppose we ought to name him," he said, stroking the white patches on his withers. The old boy flicked an ear but didn't interrupt his slow munching of a handful of oats Lucas had put in the grain box for him.

"You're better at names than me," Lucas confessed. "Like the one you picked for Bigger probably fit him as well as Sooner fits Sooner. Bigger sounds, well, bigger, just like I bet he was."

Tyler vowed someday he'd tell Lucas about the night on his way to Texas when he'd named Bigger. He'd already fed the strange black dog once, and the next evening the animal followed him again, had sneaked stealthily through the meadow grass toward his campfire, hoping for another handout.

You're bigger than I thought you'd be, Tyler remembered telling the dog, who studied him out of the same peculiar eyes he'd bequeathed to Sooner. *Bigger*—well, right from the moment he said the word out loud, Tyler knew the name fit so well there was no sense trying to come up with any other. Lucas was right: Bigger *was* bigger, especially when it came to his brave heart.

But that was the past; this was the present.

"I guess we could call this fella Old Fella, just like the Snepps did. As long as we keep feeding him, though, I bet he'd answer to Mud if we called him such!" Tyler said, laughing softly. "Maybe we ought to wait till Mama and Rosa Lee get up, so they can have a hand in this naming business, too. What d'you think, Lucas?"

Lucas nodded, pleased to be consulted, and as soon as breakfast was finished, everyone trekked back down to the cow shed for the naming event. Rosa Lee was as excited about it as she'd been about voting. From their pen, Calico and her speckled calf looked on with round, curious eyes.

"I like the name Mary Jane," Rosa Lee announced before anyone else could say a word. "Let's call him Mary Jane."

"That's not a fit name for a mule," Lucas objected. "Mary Jane is a sissy girl's name."

Rosa Lee raised her fist to give him a whack, but Mama caught her hand in midair. Tyler looked down at his sister. She still might suck her thumb, but she could get just as hot under the collar as quickly as Papa or Lucas.

"Now, miss, don't get so snippy," Mama warned, then stepped back from the mule and regarded him with a frown. "Umm, how about Magic? If this critter can help us get that hillside all tilled up, why, he'd be a magic mule, him being so old and all. What do you think?"

It was Tyler's and Lucas's turn to frown. Once again, Tyler leaned into the mule, who again braced himself and leaned back firmly. Once upon a time, Tyler knew the old boy had been accustomed to heaving himself against a harness and would be willing to do so again. He caressed the white spots on the mule's withers with his fingertips. Beneath were ridges of scar tissue that had been left there long ago.

"Folks call dogs with spots Spot, but that doesn't seem like much of a name for a mule," he mused aloud.

"Those patches you've got your hand on, Ty—what caused 'em?" Mama wanted to know.

"Probably he was put into a harness that didn't fit him or else the padding had been worn off it. It must have rubbed and rubbed, till it scraped the hide right off. Maybe it even drew blood. Then, when the hair grew back, it came in white."

"Sort of like a patch," Mama said, and reached out to touch them herself. She smiled. "Well, then, why don't we call him Patches?"

Tyler exchanged a glance with Lucas, who nodded and smiled. But Rosa Lee was puzzled. "You mean like patches in a quilt, Mama? Those kind of patches?"

"Sort of," Mama agreed. Rosa Lee smiled, too. "Patches," she echoed. "We're going to call you Patches, Patches." She stood on tiptoe to touch the white spots, and Tyler playfully covered her fingers with his. The mule flicked both ears, as if he was mildly pleased by all the attention, and kept on eating.

"Taking care of him'll be my job, all right, Ty?" Lucas said, rubbing Patches's neck.

"Sure enough," Tyler agreed. "Sometimes you can take Patches to a place along the creek where the grazing is good and stake him out," he went on. "After the weather gets cold, we'll keep a sharp eye on him and let him stay here in the shed so's he doesn't take a chill. And I was thinking, Lucas, it wouldn't hurt to walk him up and down the road a couple times a day. Just feel 'im," he invited Lucas, and paused to stroke the mule from stem to stern. "This old boy's muscles are froze hard as a plow blade because he was left to stand there behind the Snepps' barn till he dropped over dead."

Best of all, Mama herself seemed satisfied. "Well, boys, I think maybe you did all right for our three dollars after all," she said, and folded her arms against her waist. At that moment, Patches raised his tail and deposited a pile of manure on the earthen floor of the shed. Sooner inspected the steaming mound immediately, and in a moment the air was filled with an overpowering odor.

"Phew-ee!" Rosa Lee screeched, holding her nose and staggering out of the barn. Tyler took a bucket from a nail beside Ransom's old stall and handed it to Lucas.

"You and Rosa Lee go up to the field and pick whatever corn we missed on our first pass, all right? Later, we'll stake Patches up there and he can do his own picking."

Tyler watched his brother and sister trek off, then Mama stepped outside the shed while he got a pitchfork and removed Patches's fragrant memento. "I always wondered what it'd be like if we had to manage for ourselves permanently," she murmured. "With all of us pulling in the same direction, I have a feeling things are going to work out just fine, Ty."

Tyler turned and felt a familiar warmth rise swiftly to his cheeks. "It ain't permanent, Mama! I told you that before. It's only that Papa's got to work this surrender business out of his blood. When he does, well, he'll be able to come back to a family that's stuck tight and has got everything running smooth!"

His mother reached out to touch his shoulder lightly. "I know, Ty, I know," she said, sighing. "Maybe you're right. Maybe that's exactly how it'll be."

Tyler sneaked a look at her profile as she, too, turned

to watch Lucas and Rosa Lee head up the slope behind the house. There was something calm and accepting about the set of his mother's mouth. It was as if she knew something he didn't, as if she'd already made a separate peace with herself.

Suddenly, Tyler felt his cheeks grow cool. What if she'd been right when he read her thoughts about Papa yesterday? *I know your papa, son. He won't be back . . . not ever.*

Tyler shuddered and hurried back inside the cow shed to busy himself with turning Calico's calf out, then getting ready to milk. It couldn't be like Mama imagined. Papa would surely come home; he could feel it in his bones.

As the first thin streams of milk pinged against the side of the pail, Tyler could almost hear the sound of Papa's horse crossing the bridge over Sweet Creek. He rested his forehead against Calico's warm haunch. *Someday that's the way it'll be*, he promised himself. *Someday.*

Chapter Six

FOR THE MIDDAY MEAL, Mama cut some cornmeal mush left over from breakfast into thick slices, sprinkled each with salt and pepper, and fried them in bacon grease. Tyler washed his down with a cold glass of milk, then hooked his thumbs under his belt. He tipped his chair back against the wall like Papa used to do.

"Be a good idea if you'd walk Patches when you're done eating," he told Lucas. He used a splinter from a piece of kindling in the wood box to clean his teeth. Papa always did that, too. "It's as warm as it's goin' to be all day, Lucas, and like I told you this morning, the exercise will loosen up his old, cold muscles. We'll start him out once a day, then if he cottons to it, we'll try him twice."

Lucas scowled and finished off a slab of fried mush. "I figured on doin' it later," he mumbled, his mouth full. "Besides, this would be a mighty good day to go fishing."

"If you take care of Patches first, the job'll be done," Tyler said matter-of-factly. "Fishing can come after." He set his chair back in place, lifted a lid on the stove, and pitched his toothpick into the fire.

"And while you're working on Patches, I'll commence to fix up the henhouse," he added, giving his trousers a hitch. A doggone coon had dug under it and had almost clawed its way through the floor to where the chickens nested at night. Chickens and eggs wouldn't last a minute once the critter got inside. "See you outdoors, all right?"

Lucas grunted a reply, and Tyler went around to the back side of the cabin, where Papa had a workbench tucked under a lean-to roof. He rummaged around for a hammer, some nails, and a scrap of board, then headed for the henhouse. Later he'd try to find that rusty old trap Papa used for such predators—skunks, coons, possums, and the like—and would set it just before dark. Tyler didn't relish the thought of having to kill the coon, but if it came to that, why, he'd skin it, and Mama could cook it up for supper.

He'd been working on the henhouse only a few minutes when a peculiar racket coming from just beyond the cabin made Tyler raise his head in exasperation. Now what the devil was going on out there—?

He shaded his eyes to see better. Just above the vine-covered fence that paralleled the road and kept animals out of the garden, he saw Patches's frosted ears bobbing along at a lively clip. He heard the soft, rapid thunk of hoofbeats, then a shout from Lucas. "Gid up, there! Don't you hang back like some pokey old bag of bones!"

Tyler dropped his hammer and nails. He hit for the road at a dead run, Sooner hot on his heels, and loped through the garden in four-foot strides. He let the gate hang loose behind him as he burst onto the road.

"Whoa there, Lucas!" he yelled. "You're hurrying that old boy a way too fast. I bet that fella ain't moved so sprightly since he was a yearling!"

Lucas turned, startled, then flushed bright red. "You

said for me to loosen him up," he mumbled. "I couldn't see how he was goin' to get very loose just plodding along so slow, so I thought I'd just—"

Tyler realized Lucas was only trying to do the right thing. He'd overdone it, without realizing the harm he might cause Patches. "Well, I reckon you probably didn't hurt him much," Tyler said, eager to save Lucas from feeling foolish. There was no sense embarrassing him so he'd get cranky the next time he was told to pitch in and give a hand at chores.

Patches's breath came in quick, exhausted puffs. His mild brown eyes were open wide and glassy with surprise. He actually looked kind of funny, and Tyler couldn't help but smile. He soothed the old mule with a steady touch on the flank.

"Why, I think maybe you did kindle a little spark in the old gaffer," he said, laughing. Patches stared first at Lucas, then at Tyler, and next at Sooner as if he were truly awake for the first time since he'd arrived at Sweet Creek.

"Lookit that, Lucas—for once he ain't going straight back to sleep! But I think he's had enough exercise for this morning, so whyn't you put him back in the pen. Then you come give me a hand boarding up that hole in the chicken house."

He watched Lucas lead Patches away to the small pasture he shared with Calico and her calf. Lucas dropped his head low and studied the ground as if he were searching for something he'd just lost. There was a granitelike cast to his jaw that made Tyler groan silently.

"Lucas seems a whole lot different since I came back from Texas," Tyler confided to Sooner when his brother was out of earshot. "I had an adventure myself on that long trip to the border, but without ever leaving home, I guess

Lucas had one of his own." Sooner leaned against his knee, and Tyler reached down to rub the pup's ears. "Lucas was head of the house then, Sooner. Had to take care of Mama and Rosa Lee. Reckon you could say staying behind made him just as different as going away made me."

When Lucas joined him to mend the henhouse, Tyler made up his mind to talk about things that were safe. Not about Papa or the past. Not about Patches. Not about anything that happened on the way down to or back up from Texas.

"Remember what Mr. Snepp told us the other day, Lucas?"

"He talked about a lot of stuff," Lucas muttered.

"I mean about how maybe we should try growing some hemp."

"What about it?" Lucas grumbled sullenly.

"I was thinking maybe I ought to find out more about that. I suppose a good place to start would be to ask Uncle Matt."

"What's Uncle Matt know about hemp?" Lucas snapped, unwilling to let go of his sour frame of mind. "He's a storekeeper, not a farmer. All he does is sell stuff. Pots and pans and flour and salt and sugar and such like. What's *he* goin' to know about hemp?"

"Well, I bet he hears a lot of talk there in his store, Lucas. From folks who come in, wanting this and that, and who stop to gab awhile. If something new is happening anywhere around this neck of the woods, I'll bet Uncle Matt would be one of the first to know about it. Maybe I ought to go on down to New Hope soon as we get the fall chores done."

Lucas kept his head bent and said nothing. "Say, you want to go down there with me?" Tyler asked, as if the invitation were the most natural thing in the world.

Lucas glanced up quickly, his black eyes narrow, as if he suspected Tyler intended to play a trick on him.

"We could go together, just you and me," Tyler said, reading his brother's look. "That's what brothers are s'posed to do. You know, try to figure things out together." Lucas's smile was tentative at first, then became wide and bright. Tyler was sure he knew one thing about Lucas: He was quick to be wrathful, but just as quick to get over it. He wasn't like Papa in that respect; he wasn't the kind who'd hold a grudge forever and ever.

"I surely would like that!" Lucas exclaimed. "And it'll give me a chance to see Cousin Clayton, just like you did when you went to look for Papa." His eyes gleamed with anticipation. "When do you aim to go, Ty?" It was plain he was ready to set out first thing in the morning if need be.

"There's plenty to do here right now," Tyler cautioned. "We got all those potatoes and carrots to put up. We'll tackle that woodpile, too. Maybe we could go after Thanksgiving sometime. We'll even do Christmas errands for Mama in New Hope, if she wants us to."

"That'll be swell," Lucas said, his sunny old self again. Tyler laid his hand lightly on his brother's shoulder. Long ago, Papa laid his hand on *my* shoulder, Tyler remembered. It had mattered a lot; now, he hoped his own touch would mean as much to Lucas.

The rest of the week, Tyler and Lucas worked from early morning till dark to get the potatoes harvested and taken to the root cellar that had been dug into the hillside behind the house. Next, carrots were dug up, then turnips, parsnips, and rutabagas were carried into the cellar. Tyler covered the separate piles of produce with fresh, moist sand he and Lucas carried up from the creek, and slowly the cellar filled with the rich aroma of vegetables and damp earth. Next, they chopped wood until a mountain of it was piled up beside the cabin, ready for use when the weather got cold.

In the house, Mama and Rosa Lee peeled apples by the basketful, and all day long the kitchen was fragrant with the spicy aroma of apple butter simmering on the stove. One day Tyler beheaded several of what Mama called her over-the-hill hens. She scalded them in water heated over a fire in the yard, plucked them, cut them into pieces, then placed the chunks—fried, and glossy in their own rich gravy—in glass jars.

At night Tyler felt tired and happy, both at the same time. His back ached, yet knowing that the winter was being hedged against made him feel truly grown up. It was what Papa had wanted, he told himself each night as he drifted off to sleep.

Finally, all the chores were done, and there was even a little time left over to do something that wasn't all drudgery. One afternoon, before Sweet Creek became laced with ice at its edges, Tyler got out the fishing poles. Lucas had wanted to fish; well, this was a perfect day to do exactly that. When he checked the yard, though, he couldn't see his brother anywhere. He would have asked Rosa Lee, who usually tagged after Lucas like a shadow, but she was taking her nap in Mama's big bed in the back room.

"You know where that boy went, Mama?" Tyler asked. Mama looked up from the crust she was rolling out for a pie and shook her head.

"You've kept him awful busy lately, Ty. Most likely he's decided to take a few minutes to play somewhere. He's still only a boy," she added, as if she needed to apologize for Lucas. "Just holler that you've got the poles ready and he'll come running quick enough."

Tyler went outside and looked around for Sooner. The pup—of course, he was looking less like a pup every day, was getting so long-legged and showed promise of being both taller than Bigger and even deeper through the chest—was nowhere to be seen, either.

Tyler smiled. It made him feel mighty good to know Sooner and Lucas were off doing something together. It meant the pup was going to be a real family dog, a friend to all of them. Not like Bigger, who could be loyal only to one person at a time.

Tyler cupped his hands around his mouth and was about to give Lucas a yell when he noticed how intently Patches, who was staked out near the creek, was looking toward the cow shed. The old boy's head was up; his ears were pricked forward attentively.

Why, he hears something going on in there, Tyler realized. He eased himself noiselessly down the narrow path toward the shed. He stepped lightly into its mellow gloom, curious as to what he'd find. He froze in his tracks. What he saw made his blood go cold.

Lucas had blocked up the end of Ransom's old stall with boards, and Sooner was a prisoner inside. Lucas was hunkered down on his haunches and had a sharp stick in his hand. Tentatively, he poked at Sooner through the slats of the stall. At first Sooner seemed to think it was a new pastime. He nipped playfully at the stick, dodging it as nimbly as a flea.

Then Lucas poked at him more purposefully. Sooner began to whine, as if to complain that he was tired of playing the strange new game. He backed himself into a corner of the stall, his snowy white bib glowing in the dim light, but Lucas jabbed at him even more vigorously.

Tyler heard Sooner snap at the stick. His teeth clicked on empty air, then after another poke he started to growl.

It was the same ominous, deep-throated growl Tyler remembered coming out of Bigger's chest whenever he was threatened. *Sooner was Bigger's son.* He was bound to react to torment exactly as his father had. It was the kind of treatment that would turn him into the same dangerous renegade Bigger had been.

"Lucas!" Tyler yelled, startled at the power of his own voice.

In a single smooth, swift motion, he leaped forward and snatched the stick out of Lucas's hand. He broke it over his knee and threw it down. He wrenched the boards away from the end of the stall so Sooner could escape. With a yip, the pup skedaddled out into the sunshine, his red coat blazing like a torch through the gloom of the shed. As he flew past, Tyler saw that Sooner's brown eye was filled with bewilderment, while the pale eye was cloudy with outrage.

Tyler seized Lucas around the shoulders and hauled him outside, too. "You doggone crazy knotheaded fool!" he shouted. "What in the world were you tryin' to do in there?"

Lucas's eyes were black slits in his white face. At first Tyler thought he was frightened, then realized his brother was mad enough to chew up nails and spit out tacks.

"I ain't a fool! Ain't no knothead, either!" Lucas hissed through clenched teeth. "I just wanted Sooner to be like Bigger, so's he'd guard me like you said Bigger guarded you all the time!"

"Sooner will do just as good a job of guarding *all* of us if we treat him proper," Tyler snapped. "There's no need to pester him and make a monster out of him."

"You think you know everything!" Lucas threw back. "Just because you're the only one who got to see Papa again—"

"Cut it out, Lucas!" Tyler warned. "We already been through all this. I didn't go down to Texas to look for Papa just for the heckuvit. I would've taken you along if there'd been any way I could have, but somebody had to stay behind to take care of Mama and Rosa Lee."

"You ain't been the same since you got home," Lucas spit out, madder now than ever. "You think you're smarter'n any boy alive. Leaning your chair back after you eat like Papa used to! Picking your teeth like Papa did! Somehow you figure you got the right to order me around and always be tellin' me what to do—"

Tyler tried to explain he'd never intended to be bossy, but Lucas was in no mood for explanations.

"'Lucas, get to work on the chicken house,'" his brother mimicked, and the bitterness in his voice made Tyler draw back. "'Lucas, go walk Patches.' 'Lucas, put up the potatoes.' 'Lucas, chop wood.' Lucas, do this; Lucas do that," Lucas ranted. "Well, mister, I'm plumb tired of takin' orders from you!"

Lucas glared, his jaw set, fists bunched at his sides. No doubt about it, he was ready for battle. "You ain't Papa," Lucas finished, "you're only my brother. No way do I have to do what you say!"

"Lucas, I'm not trying to be Papa," Tyler said. He could hear the energy leak out of his voice, like feathers out of an old pillow that needed a new tick. Suddenly, he felt worn out. Truth was, it had been hard work trying to do what Papa asked—to take care of the whole family.

"Nobody can be Papa except Papa," Tyler admitted. "I'm just doing what needs to be done, that's all. Papa said for me to look after you and Rosa Lee and Mama, and that's all I'm tryin' to do, Lucas."

"How do *I* know what Papa said?" Lucas sneered. "I never got to see him again. You're the only one!" Scarlet spots burned on Lucas's cheeks like coals in a grate, and Tyler could plainly see his brother had worked himself up to a full head of steam. Lucas reached down, scooped up a rock, then cocked his arm back to hurl it.

"Put that down, Lucas. Right now," Tyler said in an even, steely voice. "You and me can't be fighting like this. It's not what Papa—"

Before he could finish, Lucas let loose. The stone zinged so close to his ear that Tyler felt a breeze lift his hair. He made a dive for Lucas's legs, tackled him around the knees, and brought him crashing to the ground with a jarring thunk.

I was wrong, Tyler realized. *Lucas does hold a grudge, and just like Papa he'll hold it forever if I don't knock it out of him right this minute.*

Lucas wiggled out of Tyler's grip and leaped to his feet. He swung a haymaker, and Tyler ducked just in time to miss it. He crouched and circled Lucas warily. He feinted as if he intended to run off toward the house, then dodged quickly behind his brother. He grabbed Lucas hard, pinning his arms to his sides.

Lucas kicked backward, landing a painful blow to Tyler's shin bone, but Tyler held on. Lucas squirmed and yelled, and they both fell to the ground. Tyler still didn't let go, even though he got a hard blow to his other shin. More than anything, he didn't want to have to haul off and clobber Lucas like he was some kind of enemy.

Instead, he squeezed his brother so hard he forced the breath right out of him. Gasping and choking, Lucas finally began to cry. His tears were the same rusty kind he'd cried in the middle of the road going over to the Snepps' place a couple weeks ago. This time, though, he cried so long and hard he finally started to hiccup. Tyler softened his grip slowly, and between hiccups and sobs, Lucas gasped out his pain.

"He was my papa, too. . . . I loved him as much as anybody . . . except he's been gone so long . . . and I was so little when he left. . . . Sometimes I'm not exactly sure I can remember what he looked like . . . or if he loved me too. . . ."

Tyler cradled Lucas as best he could, which wasn't easy seeing as how they were both nearly the same size now. At last, they flopped on their backs and stared at the sky overhead. The November sunshine was too pale and thin to have much warmth, and far above a red-tailed hawk circled and cried piercingly. Tyler remembered there'd been a hawk wheeling against the hard, blue sky above the Rio Grande the last time he saw Papa.

"He loved you in his fashion, Lucas, same's he loved all of us," Tyler said. "And I truly wish you could've gone to Texas with me, only that's not how it worked out. But as long as we live, Lucas, you and me will be brothers. *Brothers,* hear me? We can't turn on each other. We're the only men Mama and Rosa Lee got left, and we have to stick together, no matter what."

Tyler reached for his brother's hand. It was sticky because Lucas had just wiped it across his runny nose.

"Oh, Papa," Lucas said in the smallest, most forlorn voice Tyler had ever heard.

Overhead, the hawk wheeled in ever-wider arcs, and its sharp cry reminded Tyler of something breaking. Lucas's heart, maybe. His own, too.

Chapter Seven

IT SNOWED A WEEK BEFORE CHRISTMAS. Tyler woke to see the high window in the sleeping loft was covered with frost on the inside. His nose was cold, and his fingers tingled. Beside him, Lucas stirred, then he stared up at the frosted window, too.

"Doggone it," he muttered. "Means we can't go down to New Hope today like we planned." Lucas blew on his hands to warm them, raising a halo of vapor around his head. He gave a disgusted groan, then burrowed deeper under the quilts.

Tyler rolled off his side of the pallet and searched for his socks before he set his feet on the cold plank floor. "There's something else we could do today, though," he told Lucas through chattering teeth. Dried sweat made his socks as stiff as a pair of shingles, but finally he got them on. He pulled his shirt over his head, shivering to warm the space between the cloth and his ribs.

"This would be a good time to see if we can get us a deer, Lucas. We'll be able to track one real easy in that new snow." The fresh white blanket would muffle their footfalls through the woods, too. Until now Tyler had held off mentioning a hunt, knowing that if he and Lucas went crunching through the fallen leaves on a dry day, it would be the same as telegraphing their approach. Deer would get the message and scatter long before he and Lucas ever got close enough to get a decent shot.

Sooner, who started sleeping upstairs after the big battle outside the cow shed, stirred himself from where he'd been curled in a tight ball at the end of the pallet. He nuzzled a wet nose behind Tyler's ear and seemed to understand that something interesting was about to happen. Tyler hugged him and kissed the young dog on the sleek, smooth triangle between his strange-colored eyes (which he would've been too embarrassed to do if anyone was watching).

"Huh! And just how do you figure to get a deer?" Lucas snorted, his words muffled by the covers. "You know dang well Papa took his rifle with him. You aim to lasso one, or what?" The humorous prospects of such a sight tickled him, and he snickered loudly.

"He left that old Hawken behind," Tyler reminded Lucas. "I came across it the other day when I was lookin' for a trap to set outside the henhouse to catch that coon. It looked pretty rusty, but if I could get it cleaned up and can find some balls and powder and primer—well, can't tell, we might get lucky."

Lucas peered out of his cocoon of quilts, suddenly interested. "What do *you* know about powder and primer and such?"

"I watched whenever Papa got ready to go hunting," Tyler said. "Even went with him once." Then, remembering the fight with Lucas, he added quickly, "It's only because you were so little back then that Papa didn't take you, too."

Lucas inched himself out into the cold room. "I'll

help you," he offered, and groped for his own stiff socks. "Venison would taste mighty good, wouldn't it, Ty?" He shivered and smacked his lips with anticipation.

Tyler glanced swiftly at his brother, then turned away to hide a smile. It'd only been ten days since he and Lucas had their big foofaraw, but his brother had gotten over it. It was as if Lucas understood why it had to be.

Downstairs, Mama had wedges of bread already toasting facedown on top of the woodstove and soon piled them on a plate. Slathered with apple butter and washed down with hot tea, they tasted fine on such a cold morning. "Lucas and me aim to go hunting today, Mama," Tyler announced. "If we get us a deer, it'll give us a nice change from so much salt pork."

Mama flashed him a startled glance. "You're going hunting?" she echoed. "But you've never—"

"I know I've never gone by myself, Mama," Tyler admitted. "Didn't do much except traipse behind Papa once or twice." He'd been little then, not more than nine or ten, but he remembered so well the things Papa told him. "And if Papa were here right now, this is exactly the kind of day he'd go out himself, so that's what me and Lucas are going to do." When Mama smiled, Tyler knew he'd put her worry to rest.

As soon as he finished eating, Tyler retrieved Papa's old deer rifle from where he'd found it high on two pegs above the workbench out back. Papa must have been aiming to clean it up himself before he rode off with General Shelby because it wasn't like him to leave such a weapon outdoors where it'd be subject to thievery or abuse by the elements. He hadn't taken it with him because when rumors of war began to wash across the countryside in waves, Papa sent off to New Haven, Connecticut, for a fancy new repeating rifle. That had been a mighty handsome weapon, Tyler remembered, with its short barrel and a magazine that held seven cartridges.

By comparison, the old Hawken looked mighty poor when Tyler laid it on the kitchen table. He hefted it. It wasn't light, either; he judged it weighed at least ten pounds. Its .35-caliber barrel, nearly forty inches long, was rusted inside and out, and its walnut stock was scarred and badly needed polishing.

The heel of the stock, curved to fit a man's shoulder comfortably (*but would it fit a boy's?*), was protected with brass plates, and a ramrod for tamping down the charge was held securely beneath the barrel in specially designed brackets. The rifle's sights were low, and the barrel accepted a half-ounce lead ball, enough to bring down even a bear, if need be.

With Lucas at his side, Tyler set about refurbishing the Hawken with gun oil Papa had left behind. Then he rummaged in Papa's stuff for lead balls, gunpowder, and primer. Lucas watched the proceedings with increasing impatience.

"D'you have to take so blame long, Ty?" he complained. "We ought to be out there huntin' right now!"

"Ain't no rush," Tyler said. "Late in the afternoon— that's when deer like to come out to feed. Then we won't have go lookin' for 'em. They'll be right there, waiting for us." He glanced down at Sooner, who had long since given up paying attention to the conversation and had curled himself up in his favorite spot next to the wood box.

"We can't take Sooner, though," Tyler said. "He'd set off the minute he caught the scent of a deer, and we wouldn't see hide nor hair of any around here for a month."

More than worrying what Sooner might do, though,

Tyler harbored an uneasy dread that he couldn't confess to anyone, least of all to Lucas. Truth was, he'd never actually killed anything before. If you didn't count those over-the-hill chickens he helped Mama behead a few weeks ago, that is.

Tyler smoothed the pungent gun oil along the rifle barrel, then polished it with a soft cloth Mama gave him. Sometimes, when he was out doing chores and saw deer watching him from the woods, he stopped to admire them. They were elegant creatures—legs slim as reeds, their coats red as foxes in summer, their eyes limpid with gentle curiosity.

As he rubbed the rifle barrel slowly and carefully, Tyler imagined the lead ball he intended to load into the Hawken tearing through the heart or head of such an animal. The blood would gush forth to splatter the snow with scarlet . . . the animal might utter a heart-stopping death cry. Such images made his hands cool and damp.

Of course, it didn't bother everyone to kill a living creature. It sure hadn't bothered that man a whit to shoot Bigger square in the chest. Tyler shuddered to remember how quickly the light had faded from Bigger's peculiar eyes. It would fade in the same way from the mild brown eyes of a deer if he killed one today. How would he feel when it did?

Toward late afternoon, as the bare field behind the house lost its golden glow and took on cool blue tones, Tyler and Lucas pulled on extra socks, their warm coats and caps, and set out. Before leaving, Tyler took Sooner's face in his mittens, leaned close, and tried to explain why he couldn't come along. Sooner listened attentively, his brown eye hopeful, the blue one skeptical, then complained bitterly when Tyler shut the door in his face.

Tyler glanced down at the Hawken as he and Lucas

trudged silently along. Barrel and stock gleamed, and the weight of the rifle in the crook of his right arm made him feel more man than boy. And the moment of an actual killing? Tyler steeled himself and put it out of his mind.

Lucas was the first to spy the set of tracks in the snow. "Looks like a good-sized one," he whispered, pointing. Both boys scanned the edge of the field, hoping for sight of the animal. "A buck, maybe," Lucas added hopefully. "A big one, if we're lucky."

They paused, studying the distant woods that bordered the picked-over cornfield. "There he is," Tyler said finally. "See, against the trees." The deer wore its winter coat of soft gray, just about the color of the leafless tree branches, and was almost invisible. It browsed with its head down, and Tyler couldn't be sure if he saw a set of antlers. Lucas peered hard. "Yep, I see it now, too," he whispered.

The deer was a long way off, at least a hundred yards. But Papa said the Hawken had a good range, much better than an old long-barreled Kentucky rifle such as Uncle Matt kept in his store. Tyler set his legs wide apart to brace himself against the Hawken's kick, then slowly lifted the rifle, settling and resettling the brass-plated stock against his shoulder till it fit comfortably.

The deer spotted them. It raised its head and watched with the same mild, unblinking stare that Tyler had admired in the past. He aimed for a point below the crest of the animal's shoulder, up from its front elbow, where he judged its heart ought to be. The Hawken had two triggers, the first one a "set" trigger, which eased the pressure on the main trigger just in front of it and allowed for an easier let-off.

Tyler sighted carefully, set the first trigger, then squeezed down gently—*gently!*—on the second.

The blast rocked him back on his heels and made Lucas cower, his ears covered. The deer leaped up against the grillwork of bare gray tree branches, then headed for the deep woods. A moment later Tyler saw it stumble, right itself, then plunge on. A few steps later the animal stumbled again, fell, and struggled valiantly to rise. It did and kept going even deeper into the woods.

"Hurry!" Tyler yelled to Lucas. "We don't want him to get away. He's hurt bad, and if we don't get him now, the wolves surely will take care of him tonight." Together, he and Lucas floundered through the snow toward the edge of the field. There was no sign of the deer. Then Tyler found bright droplets of blood and followed the trail. He shuddered to think he might have to shoot it a second time, up close, while it watched him.

The droplets became large splatters. It was plain from the stained snow that the deer had fallen again, righted itself, and staggered on. Two minutes later they came upon a single large pool of blood, and Tyler looked up to see the animal several yards away. It was down for the last time, next to a fallen log. As he and Lucas approached, the buck got part way to its knees, then collapsed into the snow, its neck extended, its mouth open. Tyler's heart hammered under his jacket with a mixture of relief and regret.

By the time he and Lucas got to its side, the young buck's eyes had already lost their sheen. Twin ribbons of steam rose from its flaring nostrils. A moment later a froth of pink foam bubbled around its mouth, then a death shudder riddled all four limbs.

"He's only got a single point," Lucas muttered, disappointed.

"What we've got to do now is get it home so we can gut it and hang it up to cure properly," Tyler said. He avoided the pronoun *he,* which seemed too personal. Lucas helped loop a rope around the animal's hind legs, then they proceeded to drag the carcass home. It took every ounce of their strength, but once they got out into the snow-covered field, the going was easier. Tyler resisted glancing back over his shoulder. He knew a wide, bright pink swath would be left in the snow, and he didn't want to see it.

My first deer, he thought. In spite of how quickly the light had faded from the animal's eyes, it was hard not to be halfway proud. There'd be extra meat on the table for many meals—fresh liver and venison roasts and chops for Mama to cook, and now she could make mincemeat pies with real meat in them.

He'd done something else a grown man could do, Tyler reflected. Papa would never had any cause to complain about how the family was being taken care of. It meant a certain young buck would never wander through the woods again, but as he hauled against the rope, it occurred to Tyler that sometimes you had to trade one thing for another in order to keep a family going. Today a little death had been traded for a little life.

For the next several days it snowed every afternoon. Snow piled up on the porch, and frost built up on the inside of all the windows in the house. On Christmas Day Mama put a haunch of venison in the oven, and the kitchen was filled with the delicious smell of roasting meat. During the holiday no classes were held at Two Mile school; just the same, Tyler sat at the table and worked on the geography lesson Mr. Blackburn had assigned, while Lucas did his sums.

To keep herself busy, Rosa Lee pushed Papa's chair

closer to the four-paned window where he used to sit. She began to carve designs on the thick white covering with the edge of her thumbnail. She hummed as she made round circles for people's faces and put in dots for eyes and crescent moons for smiles.

"I'll make a face for Sooner, too," she said. Alas, his ears turned out to be enormous, bigger even than his head, so she scrubbed out the pup's portrait with the heel of her hand. She pressed her nose to the glass and peered out through the hole she'd made in the frost.

"I see somebody coming up the road," she announced. She said it as if people came up the road every day, but the kitchen instantly fell into stunned silence.

"Wait. There's two somebodies," Rosa Lee added, as cool as a cucumber. "One's taller than the other one."

Nobody else said a word. Even the teakettle seemed to withhold its singing. Tyler, Lucas, and Mama hurried to the window themselves. For a split second Tyler was grateful that he'd figured out how to use the Hawken. He'd be able to protect the family in case scalawags had decided to come nosing around the place. He fetched the rifle from where he'd stashed it behind the door of Mama's bedroom and laid it across the table, ready for the worst.

Before allowing himself to get too panicky, Tyler lifted Rosa Lee aside and peered through the peephole himself. There were, indeed, two figures approaching the far side of the bridge that crossed Sweet Creek. It was exactly as she reported: One of them was taller than the other.

The tall one . . . Tyler swallowed hard and automatically touched his breastbone. An erratic rattling had commenced in his chest. The tall one was almost tall enough to be Papa. . . .

But why would Papa be traveling with a companion—and strangest of all, why would he be traveling on foot? Papa had ridden away alone, on horseback; why wouldn't he come home the same way? Tyler squinted, then turned his attention to the smaller of the two figures and studied it closely.

He couldn't believe his eyes. "Why, doggone—it's Cousin Clayton!" he exclaimed. "Last time I was in New Hope—you know, when I went down there to get Sooner from Uncle Matt—well, I invited Clayton to come up to see us. But what possessed that boy to pick such terrible weather to accept the invitation?"

Lucas and Rosa Lee jostled for their turn at the peephole. "Let me see again," Rosa Lee insisted, elbowing her way into position. "I'm the one who saw 'em first—besides, it's *my* peephole!" But Tyler held on to his place a moment longer.

His attention was drawn back to Clayton's companion. It couldn't be Uncle Matt, who was on the short side. Besides, Uncle Matt walked with a limp because he'd had an accident at a sawmill when he was only a boy. He had a wooden leg on account of it, and it was the reason he'd never gone off to war like Papa.

Just the same, there was something hauntingly familiar about the way the stranger carried himself. Tall, though not as tall as Papa, he walked with a loose, easy grace. Not stiffly like a man who'd lived on horseback, as Papa had. The pair were halfway across the bridge before Tyler finally realized who the second traveler was.

"Why, it's Isaac Peerce," he murmured softly. Disbelief made his voice sound hollow against the windowpane.

"You mean the Isaac Peerce you met when you went lookin' for Papa?" Lucas asked, doubt causing his voice to change pitch. "The one who gave you a lump on your head with his slingshot? *That* Issac Peerce?"

"The same," Tyler said again, still unable to believe what his own eyes told him was true. A welcome gladness filled up the places inside that so often felt empty, places Tyler despaired would ever be full again. "The same Isaac Peerce . . ."

Chapter Eight

TYLER LEFT THE HAWKEN ON THE TABLE, flung the door open, and flew out onto the road. Lucas and Rosa Lee followed hot on his heels. He ran toward the bridge, unmindful of the chill air or the snow under his sock feet. Sooner was the last one out of the cabin but passed them all, barking at the top of his voice.

"Ain't you boys a sight!" Tyler cried. "Who'd expect the likes of you to come calling in weather like this!"

Isaac's smile was as wide and shy as Tyler remembered, but for a moment it was Cousin Clayton who captured his attention. He stood a lot taller and straighter now, and darned if some of the little-boy tallow hadn't melted off his bones, giving him a few sharp edges. He finally looked like a boy his age ought to.

Clayton stuck out his hand, and when Tyler reached for it, his cousin's grip was firm. "Bet you never thought I'd do it!" Clayton chortled. As much as he'd changed, though, Tyler noted that in Clayton's pale face, his small brown eyes still resembled two raisins stuck in a wad of unbaked bread dough.

"When Isaac showed up down at the store and told us

he was looking for you, I figured it was time. You know my mama, though," Clayton said with a sigh. "She cried and carried on and wouldn't turn loose of me till Papa told her she had to." Tyler nodded. Clayton being an only child, it was natural that Aunt Margaret would be eager to hang on to her darling boy forever.

Tyler turned slowly to Isaac. The angry scar that streaked like a red lightning bolt across Isaac's dark cheek was somewhat paler now, but his chipped-tooth smile was as familiar as when they'd first met on the way to Texas many months ago.

"Never figured to see you again in this life," Tyler said softly. He held out his hand, which was nearly swallowed up in Isaac's larger paw.

"There's a law now that says I'm a freedman," Isaac told him with a cocky toss of his head. "Can't nobody call me a runaway or haul me back anyplace I don't want to be." Then his glance turned sly. "Not that one of the things I aimed to do—being a freedman an' all—was to come lookin' for *you!* It were something a man in New Orleens gave me that put that in my head!"

Tyler drew his brows together. "A man in New Orleans put you in mind to look me up?"

Isaac took a deep breath and seemed about to explain, then he glanced uneasily at Lucas and Rosa Lee. "It be a long story, Ty," he murmured. "Too long to tell in the middle of this here bridge with sech a cold wind blowin'." He clamped his jaw shut, and Tyler realized it was the presence of his brother and sister that suddenly changed Isaac's mind about saying another word.

There'll be lots of time for stories later, Tyler told himself. Anyway, the snow had soaked through his socks, and the wind Isaac mentioned cut through his thin shirt. Tyler eagerly hustled the visitors toward the cabin.

"You boys come on in and join us for Christmas dinner," he invited grandly, the same way Papa did whenever folks showed up at mealtime. He waved Clayton and Isaac through the kitchen door, pleased that the cabin was so warm and filled with the smell of roasting meat.

"Lucas and me got us a deer a few days ago, and Mama is cooking up a haunch as we speak," Tyler boasted. "We got a whole root cellar full of stuff—taters and carrots and rooty-beggars—you can count on there bein' plenty to eat at our table!" He felt his chest swell to know how much the family had to offer in times that still were lean for others. But when Tyler asked Rosa Lee to set out two more plates, Mama abruptly got as flustered as a setting hen.

It was true the family hadn't had company to speak of in all the years since Papa went away, yet Tyler had never seen her act so skittish. She glanced from Isaac to Clayton and back again, then crooked a finger at Tyler and beckoned him into the back room.

"Son, I don't believe we can all sit down for supper together," she whispered, her arms crossed firmly.

"Why not, Mama?" Then it dawned on him. "Why, shoot! No need for you to worry, Mama. I already thought about us not having chairs enough to go around. I know we've only got four, plus Rosa Lee's stool—so I'll just draw me up a chunk of oak that Lucas and me haven't split up yet for the wood box. It'll do me fine, Mama—"

"Son, that's not what I meant at all," she interrupted. Tyler was amazed to see that his mother had set her mouth in a thin, hard line. "I'm not talking about chairs, Tyler. Nossir, I'm not talking about who sits on what."

"Then what *are* you talking about, Mama? I saw the size of that venison roast you stuck in the oven this afternoon. It's a special holiday, and we've got enough in our root cellar to feed the whole Iron Brigade if it showed up!"

"Tyler, it's on account of . . ." Mama hesitated, then nibbled on her lower lip as she often did when she was upset. "It's on account of that other boy."

"Other boy? You talkin' about Isaac, Mama?"

"Yes, son, I most surely am." Tyler saw his mother draw herself up and square her shoulders. It was plain she was relieved to have spoken her mind. She smoothed her apron in the stern way she did in the old days when Papa came home from McMinnville smelling sweetly of liquor.

"Unless you have gone blind, Tyler, you can plainly see he's a black boy. Black and white don't eat together, son. It wouldn't be fitting to sit down at the same table with folks like him."

Tyler let the words sink in. *Folks like him.*

Well, it surely was true he'd never seen Uncle Matt sit down at the same table with his hired man, Henry. Henry had his own place out back and sometimes Aunt Margaret took food out to him, but mostly Henry cooked his own. Even had himself a little garden where he grew sweet potatoes, melons, and corn. Kept a few chickens, too. More than once, Tyler had caught a whiff of a delicious smell coming from Henry's little cabin behind the livery barn down there in New Hope, had heard Henry singing to himself.

Yet he couldn't deny that Henry never sat down at Uncle Matt's table, and Uncle Matt never sat at Henry's. That was before the war, though. Mr. Lincoln had turned the whole country upside down so black folks didn't have to be slaves anymore—even got killed himself in the process—so didn't that mean everyone had to set their feet on a different path now?

"Mama, Isaac's goin' to eat with us tonight," Tyler said in a steady voice. He didn't want to quarrel with her, but settling the matter was a little bit like having to give Lucas a drubbing. It was something that had to be done. Now.

"I went and got that deer for us, Mama, and I aim we should share it with Isaac just as much as we share it with Cousin Clayton." Mama turned her mouth down and stared at the floor, as if in assent. Tyler knew better. Something else still needed to be said.

"You're right about Isaac bein' black, Mama. Can't make him white, now can I, no more'n I can trade my own skin for his. But that black boy was a friend to me when I needed one, and now I aim to be the same right back to him."

Mama wagged her head with disapproval. She didn't look pretty with that scowl on her face and her mouth so pinched. Tyler was relieved when she finally shrugged and gave her apron a flick as if she'd just spied flour dust on it.

"Well, you're right about the deer," she admitted. "You're the one who got it, sure enough. Can't argue with you about that. I guess it's yours to share however you want." She frowned. "But it don't seem right that white folks and black ones should take on as if there's no difference at all between 'em!"

"Maybe there's not as much difference as you think, Mama," Tyler said. He didn't know which surprised him more: the set of his own mind or his mother's reluctant hospitality. Someday he'd tell her how Isaac got that scar on his face. He'd tell her what had happened to Isaac's mama and daddy. Hadn't she used the phrase *on our own*? Lordy—who was more on his own than Isaac?

"And where do you aim to have him sleep tonight?" Mama demanded, not ready to give up yet. "Down there in the shed, I hope."

"Nope, Mama. Isaac is goin' to sleep right here in the house where it's warm, right along with Cousin Clayton." Tyler took his mother's arm and gently steered her back to the kitchen. "Unless you want to stick Clayton down there in the shed along with Isaac," he whispered, smiling. "But if you send Aunt Margaret's darling boy out to sleep in a cold cow shed, she'll never let you hear the end of it!"

At supper, there were heaping bowls of golden corn, snowy mountains of mashed potatoes, and carrots glazed with brown sugar. Slices of roast venison swam in their own dark gravy, and Tyler noticed in the lamplight that the faces of everyone around the table seemed ruddy—neither black nor white. Mama served up apple pie, too, and Clayton declared Aunt Margaret had never baked a better one. The compliment made Mama squeeze out her first smile of the whole evening.

"Now what's that about some fella in New Orleans?" Tyler asked Isaac.

"Oh, it be a long story, like I said," Isaac replied. "I could use some sleep after all this traveling. Let's save that till tomorrow."

So while Mama and Rosa Lee cleaned up the dishes, Tyler busied himself unrolling a couple of old corn-husk pallets that were kept stacked in a corner of the sleeping loft.

"With you boys all sleeping up yonder," Mama called up the stairs, "I'll keep Rosa Lee downstairs with me." The announcement made Rosa Lee whoop and dance around the table as if it was the best holiday ever. Sleeping all night in Mama's big feather bed was a treat that wasn't granted often enough to suit her.

Clayton and Isaac settled down on their pallets and pulled their quilts up. Tyler and Lucas climbed onto the pallet they shared, and Sooner wedged himself between them like a log.

"Can't b'leeve I finally made it to Sweet Creek on my own," Clayton murmured sleepily from his place across the room. "Before, it was always you visiting me, Ty. Now I'm the one who's come calling."

"And I be here, too," Isaac added from his spot on the opposite side of the room. "Can come and go where I want now that I'm a freedman."

Tyler smiled into the darkness and buried his fingers in Sooner's thick coat. The dog nuzzled a cool, damp nose into his palm. Funny, wasn't it? Tyler marveled. How sometimes life could turn around and seem almost good, after being bad for so long.

As soon as breakfast was finished the next morning, Lucas and Rosa Lee took Clayton down to the shed to inspect Patches, and Tyler offered to show Isaac where Bigger was buried. "He was some dawg, that Bigger," Isaac mused as they walked across the bridge. "What happened to him, Ty—and how come you got another one with those same queery eyes, one brown as an acorn, the other blue as the moon?"

"Sooner's one of Bigger's pups," Tyler explained. "Bigger put my uncle Matt's prize hound, Daisy, in the family way, and this is one of the pups she had. Not all of 'em ended up with those eyes, though. Only Sooner. Uncle Matt said he hated raising a batch of misbegot pups, but, praise the Lord, he didn't have the heart to drown 'em. So I got us a fine pup to take Bigger's place."

Side by side, Tyler and Isaac walked up the hill to

where Bigger lay beneath the frozen earth, watched over by the three bare apple trees that in a few weeks would wear gowns of white blossoms. The sun had begun to melt the snow, yet some still rimmed the curled leaves that covered the spot where Bigger slept.

Isaac listened solemnly while Tyler told about the afternoon in McMinnville when the stranger shot Bigger through the heart. He described how the blood spread across Bigger's white chest, how the light faded from his eyes. When he was through, Isaac stirred the wet leaves on the grave lightly with his toe.

"Since we be havin' such a serious conversation," he murmured when Tyler finished, "I reckon it be a good time for me to tell you about that man in New Orleens."

"Was hoping you would," Tyler said.

"Thing is, the man I met down there gave me something I knew you'd want to have."

"Sounds mighty peculiar to me!" Tyler exclaimed. "I already told you I don't know a soul in New Orleans! Never been down that way. Don't know anyone who has, not even Uncle Matt."

"Well, I headed there hoping to find some of my kin. Din't, though, so I got me a little job helping folks carry their baggage after they got off boats there at the docks," Isaac said. "One fella, he had me haul some stuff way up the street to a place he aimed to stay for the night. When I was done, he claimed he din't have no way to pay me. All he had was a trifle he said I could trade later for a little money. It wasn't a trifle, though. It was something you showed me when we were camping together, Ty. Minute I laid eyes on it, why, I knew I had to come to Missouri to give it back to you."

Tyler frowned and watched as Isaac dug in his pants pocket. "Hold out yo' hand, white boy."

"You promised not to call me that anymore," Tyler reminded him, but held his hand out, palm up. In it, Isaac placed something warm and round.

Tyler stared. It was the pale blue color as the moon on certain nights . . . the same eerie shade as one of Bigger's eyes . . . as cloudy as the eye that had been passed on to Sooner from his Highland Scots ancestors.

"It's the aggie Papa gave me for my birthday when I was eight," Tyler breathed. He'd given it back to Papa on the banks of the Rio Grande hoping it would bring him luck. Now here it was, back in his own palm. But how had it gotten to Mexico and back?

"That weren't all the man give me, either." Isaac dug deeper in his pocket. He held out a piece of paper that had been folded in quarters and whose edges were so frayed and gray Tyler knew it had traveled a long way.

"Man said this went along with the aggie but claimed he din't have no use for either one. No need to fret about me pryin' into your affairs, though," Isaac added. "On account of I don't know how to read. Bein' a field hand, I never learned nothin' about letters and such. Sometimes houseboys did, but not the likes of Isaac Peerce."

Tyler unfolded the letter slowly. The handwriting in it wasn't Papa's. It belonged to a stranger, which sent a chill down his backbone. He swallowed hard and began to read aloud.

"Dear Family, my friend William Emerson is writing this for me. Truth is, things haven't turned out like I planned. When the men heard President Andy Johnson planned to grant amnesty to deserters, the temptation to head home was too much for 'em to resist."

Tyler paused, not sure he wanted to read on. Isaac kept his glance fastened on the snowy leaves that covered Bigger's grave and waited respectfully.

"But a few of us agreed we'd still never surrender. We came on down here, all the way to South America, to a place called Brazil."

So far away! Tyler knew where Brazil was—on the right-hand edge of the southern continent, colored bright yellow on the map Mr. Blackburn kept tacked on the wall in school. And Isaac bragged about how far *he* had traveled!

"Then there was trouble," the letter continued. "A fight broke out as we were fixing to set sail for England. I got wounded in the fracas. Seemed like a no-account thing at first. Something went wrong, though. Infection set in, the doctor said, though he couldn't talk much English and I couldn't talk much Spanish, so I can't tell you much else.

"I ran out of luck, you see. Sort of like Ransom did. My, wasn't that a horse to be proud of! He went down in battle like the bravest Confederate cavalryman you ever saw." Tyler could see the smile that, wounded and sick though he was, must have lighted Papa's face as he remembered bold, red Ransom, as proud and high-headed as he was himself.

"I know I won't last much longer. So I'm giving this letter and Tyler's blue aggie to Mr. Emerson. Someday, maybe both will find their way back to Sweet Creek."

Isaac brought them home to us, Tyler wished he could tell his father. Knowing they'd arrived safely might make him rest easier. Then Papa had a few words for each member of the family.

"Ty, keep right on being accountable, just like your uncle Matt. Lucas, you're like me—don't follow orders very well— but take Tyler's word for things. Rosa Lee, grow up to be as good a woman as your mama. Wife, I should have told you oftener I loved you, because I surely did. I'm tired now, family. I pray we'll meet in the Great Beyond. Your father and husband, John Bohannon."

Tyler swallowed hard again. At the end, Papa wanted to be called just plain John Bohannon. Maybe he knew better than anyone else that the gallant gypsy, Black Jack, had died long ago, on the morning Robert E. Lee rode his fine gray horse, Traveller, to Appomattox Court House to surrender to Ulysses S. Grant.

For a while neither Tyler nor Isaac spoke. "I 'spected it weren't goin' to be good news," Isaac murmured at last. Tyler felt himself sink under the weight of Isaac's black hand on his shoulder. The news would be painful for the other three to hear, yet it would have to be told.

Tyler was sure Mama had already prepared herself. The letter would only confirm what she already knew in her heart. Rosa Lee was too young yet to fully understand that it meant Papa would never come home again. *But Lucas!*

Dreading how hard his brother would take the news, Tyler allowed himself to lean against Isaac for a moment. He hadn't cried when Papa rode across the Rio Grande and vanished into Mexico. He'd hardly cried at all when Bigger got shot through the heart in McMinnville. But now, at last, he let the tears come.

Chapter Nine

WOULD IT BE BEST TO WAIT TILL he and Lucas were alone and tell him first what had happened to Papa? Tyler asked himself as he and Isaac trudged across the bridge toward the cabin.

No, Papa belonged to the whole family. Mama and Rosa Lee deserved to hear the news at the very same time Lucas did. That way, nobody would feel left out or believe later that different words had been used for one than for the other. If everyone heard Isaac's story at once, they could all shoulder the burden of loss equally.

"Cousin Clayton and me will take a turn walkin' that old mule," Isaac offered when Tyler told him he was going to gather the family around the kitchen table and tell them the news. "This be a time folks need to themselves. Not a time for strangers listenin' in, 'specially not black ones," Isaac said.

"Your color doesn't have anything to do with it," Tyler said gruffly.

Isaac chuckled in an odd throwaway fashion that made Tyler glance at him sharply.

"Oh, but it do, it do!" Isaac exclaimed. "You think I

din't see how fussed up your mama got when I sat down to eat at your table? 'Deed I did! An' your cousin Clayton weren't none too keen on sleepin' in the same loft with the likes of me, either! The big war Mr. Lincoln fought might be over, Ty, but things between white folks and black ones be a long time gettin' sorted out."

There was no way Tyler could argue the point. As they'd climbed the stairs into the loft, Clayton had whispered with astonishment, "You mean he'll be sleeping *right in the same room* as us boys?"

"Right along with us," Tyler assured him, as if it were something that didn't need to be discussed. He knew Isaac also was right about the family sitting down together with no strangers present—not even with Cousin Clayton listening—when William Emerson's letter was read again.

After Isaac hiked off down to the pen where Patches was kept, Tyler gathered Mama and Rosa Lee together and called Lucas back to the kitchen. He sat at the head of the table and asked each of them to sit down with him. He laced his fingers together the way Mr. Blackburn did when he was explaining a new lesson. Tyler studied his thumbnails. It was hard to know exactly how or where to commence.

"Isaac didn't come all the way to Missouri to pay us a social call," he began. "He had something special to bring us."

Rosa Lee's eyes brightened. "You mean Isaac brought us a present?"

Tyler thought a moment. "Well, in a way, that's exactly what it is," he said. "It's a gift for all of us, one none of us ever expected to get." Rosa Lee smiled eagerly, her black eyes full of glee, as if in another moment Tyler intended to place a brightly wrapped package in the middle of the table.

Instead, Tyler reached into his pocket and took out the pale blue marble. He placed it on the table but it wouldn't stay put. It rolled slowly toward the left side because the floor underneath wasn't quite level. Tyler caught it just before it fell off the edge. He repositioned it securely in a slight hollow made by a knot in one of the pine planks.

Rosa Lee frowned. "*That's* the present Isaac brought us? A dumb old blue marble?" She slumped in her chair, disappointed, and stuck out her lower lip.

"It looks a lot like the aggie Papa gave you for your birthday, Ty," Lucas said, leaning forward to peer at it more intently. "A long time ago, when you were only eight, right?"

"Right, Lucas. It *is* the one Papa gave me. It's the reason Isaac came all the way up here from New Orleans, just so's he could give it back. A man on the docks down there passed it on to him because he had no way to pay Isaac for doing a chore."

"Now isn't that something!" Mama exclaimed. "I expect it means that man knew Papa."

"Yes, ma'am," Ty said, "and he gave Isaac a letter from Papa, too."

This time, it was Lucas's eyes that glowed expectantly. "Read it, Ty!" He pressed himself against the edge of the table, looking first at the marble then at Tyler. "Does he say when he's comin' home?"

For a moment Tyler considered explaining right off that's not how it was going to be. He moistened his dry lips, then decided it was best if Papa told everything in his own words. He began to read, just as he'd read the letter aloud to Isaac only an hour ago.

As Tyler heard Papa's words a second time, a peculiar calm settled on his spirit. It was a feeling he'd never had before. Maybe it came now because at last there was an end to the ending. He read slowly, knowing that Papa's farewell would cause the rest of the family the same kind of pain it had caused him. Papa's words spilled across the table and Tyler imagined they clustered around the blue marble, giving it a special glow.

". . . ran out of luck . . . won't last much longer . . . Lucas, . . . take Tyler's word for things. Rosa Lee, grow up to be as fine a woman as your mama. Wife, I should have told you oftener I loved you. . . . I'm tired now, family. I pray we'll meet in the Great Beyond. Your father and husband, John Bohannon."

Tyler laid the letter on the table, a frail, wrinkled gray square with raggedy edges. No one spoke. Rosa Lee was the first to break the silence. "Did Papa really say my name in his letter, Ty?" She wasn't six yet; it was her nature to dwell on the most obvious thing first.

"He surely did, Rosa Lee." Tyler pointed to it on the gray square. "See, there it is, spelled out nice and clear as you please. *Rosa Lee.* Just about the prettiest name there is." She smiled a little, and Tyler realized she didn't really understand that Papa was saying good-bye for the last time.

"He loved us all, though words didn't come easily to him," Mama said at last. There was a softness in her face and a faraway look in her blue eyes. Was she remembering the first time she ever laid eyes on Papa, back when they were young and just starting out, before there were any children or any war? Tyler hoped she'd always remember the words *Wife, I should have told you oftener I loved you . . .*

"When Cousin Clayton goes back to New Hope, I'll ask him to have Uncle Matt put a notice in the paper," Mama added, sighing and dabbing at the corner of her eye with the edge of her apron. "Folks for miles around always had a fondness for your papa. They'll want to know what became of him."

For a long time, Lucas said nothing at all. "It means Papa's never coming back, don't it, Ty?" he finally asked. There was a thin, stretched-out sound in his voice, like a worn-out banjo string.

"Yep, Lucas, that's what it means. Not ever," Tyler agreed. The truth couldn't be varnished over. There was no way to make it easier for Lucas to hear.

"Where d'you think he's buried, Ty?"

"Why, I suppose his friend Mr. Emerson laid him to rest right there in Brazil. At the edge of the sea, I'll wager, close by where they were fixing to sail away to England."

Lucas didn't cry. Instead, he stared out of the window, his hands resting on the tabletop, not balled up into angry fists but with fingers outstretched. Tyler saw the heartbreak in his brother's black eyes, eyes that were so much like Papa's, and wished Isaac's news had been otherwise.

That's not how life worked, though. Tyler remembered his own last glimpse of Papa, how long he'd waited for the farewell wave that never came, and remembered what he'd whispered into Bigger's ear that day.

Dreams are funny things, Bigger . . . the one Papa's got is different from mine . . . he can't let go of it . . . but I think it's time for me to turn loose of mine. . . . Now Lucas would have to find a way to turn loose of his dream, too.

"Ty, would it be all right if I took Sooner and walked up into the hills?" Lucas asked. His request was matter-of-fact, neither sorrowful nor aggrieved. "I reckon I'd like to be alone for a while."

"Sure you can, Lucas. Sooner's your dog as much as

he's mine." It was true. The matter of what happened in Ransom's old stall had been settled once and for all.

Then, Tyler and Mama and Rosa Lee watched from the porch as Lucas called Sooner from his busy work with Isaac and Clayton and set out for the top of the slope that next year might be planted with hemp. Every few steps, Sooner looked up at Lucas and waved his plumy red tail. Lucas reached down a hand to rub him behind the ears and once got down on his knees, stared into Sooner's eyes, and hugged him hard. Tyler reached a hand out to Mama and the other to Rosa Lee and gathered them close.

"Lucas will be all right," he told them. "I don't know how, but he will."

Clayton spent three more nights at Sweet Creek, then announced he was ready to head for home. Tyler told his cousin again how surprised he was by what had happened to him since they'd seen each other last.

"You've turned into a whole different person, Clayton. It's more than just the tallow melting off you. I don't think you're your mama's darling baby boy anymore!" he exclaimed. Clayton grinned smugly, as if he'd just gotten a citation for bravery in battle, then turned to Isaac.

"Soon as we get back to New Hope, Isaac, I'll bet my papa can find work for you at the store. Henry's got himself a nice little place out back, and he won't mind having company of his own kind."

Tyler saw Isaac study the floor. How did those words, *company of his own kind,* sound to him? Isaac shuffled his feet and didn't seem to know what to say.

"That's mighty kindly of you, Clayton, but I've asked Isaac to stay on here awhile," Tyler blurted. His invitation caused Mama's jaw to drop to the collar of her dress.

"Lucas and me will be needing plenty of help putting in crops soon as the weather warms up. When we run out of work here, then Isaac can go on down to New Hope—if that's what he wants to do."

Mama gave him one of her we'll-talk-about-this-later looks, then packed Clayton a lunch. He hiked off down the road and across the bridge as if he'd been traveling alone all his life. Just the same, Rosa Lee kept herself posted at the window like a sentry for two days, in case he decided to come back. When she announced that she saw someone coming up the road again, Tyler only laughed.

"Seeing Clayton and Isaac come up the road was a one-time thing, Rosa Lee," he teased, and gave one of her black curls a tug. But what if Clayton had some kind of bad luck or got scared and was headed back this way? Tyler went to the window himself and peered out. When he looked beyond the bridge, it was to see the latest traveler arriving in a light wagon drawn by a runty spotted pony and who seemed to be in a powerful hurry.

"It's Oat Snepp," he said, which was almost as big a surprise as seeing Clayton and Isaac had been. The wagon rolled across the bridge with a noisy clatter, then Oat looped the pony's reins around the gatepost in front of the cabin. He hustled through the gate, and Tyler saw right away that he was pale and distressed.

"It's my mother," Oat said, even before Tyler could ask what was wrong.

Mama, who had hurried outside, too, covered her heart with her hand. "Ah, Tyler mentioned she wasn't well," she murmured. She gently urged Oat inside the cabin, where she pressed him into a chair. She poured some sweet cider into a pan to warm and even added a piece of cinnamon stick to it. "Has Mrs. Snepp taken a turn for the worse, son?"

"Might say so," Oat answered dully, then fell silent. "She died last evening. Just about suppertime."

"Ah," Mama said again. The news came so quick on the heels of learning about Papa that Tyler had the feeling the cabin walls had heard altogether too many tales of death and dying.

"Mrs. Bohannon . . . ah . . . my father sent me over to ask if you would . . . um . . . help with washing . . . ah . . . the body and all. To get my mama ready for burial, you know. There's just us boys at home, and we don't know much about . . . um . . . how to—"

"Why, of course I will," Mama said. "That's woman's work, son, not something men take to easily." She poured the cider into a mug and set it in front of Oat. "We can head back straightaway, soon as you've finished that drink to warm your insides. I'll fix you some bread and butter, too; after all, you treated my family to a good meal at your table." Then she turned to Tyler.

"Why don't you grain Oat's horse while I get ready to go back and help the Snepps through this hard time?"

Oat sat silently at the table, holding his hands around the cider mug as if to warm them. He gulped the drink. "Might be a good time for a prayer," Mama said before she retreated to the back room to ready herself. She folded her hands and bent her head.

"Dear Lord, take care of Oat's mother, who is at your heavenly gates as we speak. Lottie Snepp was a fine woman who loved her children, and she'll be dreadfully missed by them all. Amen."

"Amen," Tyler said, as did Lucas and Rosa Lee. Hunched over his steaming cider, Oat started to sniffle. Not loudly. Not with much fuss. There wasn't any rust in his tears, as there'd been in Lucas's, only the weary crying of a boy who'd had to be a mother to his brothers too long.

Tyler sighed inwardly and went to get some grain for Oat's pony. There was no easy way to lose folks you loved. No matter how or when it happened. After a while the pain went away, but Oat would find out—just as he and Lucas already had—that sometimes when you least expected it, a stab of loss pierced your heart and the wound was as fresh as at the beginning.

By the time he got back to the kitchen, Mama had put on her best apron, wrapped her hair up tight so no straggly ends could get loose from the knot, and had a clean dress on Rosa Lee. "You three boys are going to be in charge of things till I get back," she said in a way that made Tyler understand she'd never get around to lecturing him about inviting Isaac to stay to help with crops. "Now mind you keep the kitchen tidy, and I'll be back as soon as Mrs. Snepp's funeral is over."

Tyler stood with Isaac and Lucas and watched till the wagon clattered across the bridge and vanished around the bend in the road.

"Oat's lucky," Lucas said wistfully.

"Lucky how?" Tyler asked, surprised. Did he somehow think it was easier to lose a mama from sickness than a papa in a war?

"He gets to have a funeral for his mama. We didn't get to have one for Papa."

"Well, maybe we ought to," Tyler said. The more he thought about it, the better the idea seemed. "While they're burying Mrs. Snepp over yonder, we'll have our own funeral right here."

Lucas nodded. He said he'd found a special place at the top of the long hill when he and Sooner had gone off by themselves. It was the kind of burial spot Papa might have picked for himself if he'd been able to. "You can look right down on the house from up there," Lucas murmured. "Can see the bridge . . . the road coming up to it and crossing over . . . how Sweet Creek wanders its way south . . . all the little low hills that lay between our place and the Snepps'."

"Isaac, you come, too," Tyler invited. It would be something the three of them could share while Mama and Rosa Lee were taking care of a different kind of burial.

Lucas was right: The spot he'd found was so perfect that Tyler vowed someday he'd be buried there himself. Below, the pale winter sun gleamed on the ice-edged ribbon that was Sweet Creek. In the distance, he could see the three apples trees beneath which Bigger rested.

"You be the one to say some words for Papa," Lucas suggested, "on account of I don't know any."

"Sure you do, Lucas," Tyler answered, "but I'll go first to help get you started." Isaac hung back with Sooner, both of them seeming to know this was a time brothers had to share.

Tyler folded his hands against his belt buckle. "Papa, we know your bones are a long way from this place, but we got a feeling your spirit is right here with us today." He was surprised that his voice wasn't quavery at all.

"We aim to set this little patch of ground aside for you, Papa. It was Lucas himself that picked it out for you, and someday we'll all be laid to rest here at your side."

Then Lucas folded his hands across his own belt buckle. He didn't speak right away. "Papa, it's been so long since you seen me or I seen you that we might not know each other. Only I'm pretty sure we would, on account of everyone says I look just like you. What I want you to know, Papa, is—"

Lucas halted a moment and had to swallow twice before he went on. "—is that I loved you, and Tyler says you loved me, too, even though I was too young when you left for you to give me an aggie like you gave him. From here you'll be able to see the sun come up in the morning, Papa, and watch it go down every night. Amen."

Behind them, Isaac began to sing softly in a voice that was deeper than that of most boys his age. The sound that floated past Tyler's ears was as rich and dark as molasses, and the words were perfect for Papa. It was a lively song that Tyler was sure he'd heard Henry sing as he passed by the black man's little house down in New Hope, but Isaac sang it slowly.

> *"You may bury me in the East,*
> *You may bury me in the West,*
> *But I'll hear the trumpet sound*
> *In-a-that morning, in-a-that morning . . ."*

The words drifted over the valley below, over the roof of the cabin, skimmed the surface of the silver-edged creek. Tyler draped his arm around Lucas's shoulders. Papa would have liked Isaac's song.

"Rest well, Papa," Lucas said softly.

"Rest well," Tyler echoed.

At last, John Bohannon was home to stay.

Chapter Ten

THEY WERE ONLY HALFWAY DOWN the slope after committing Papa's spirit to the hilltop when Tyler heard a strange noise below. He cocked his head. It seemed to be coming from near the cow shed.

He threw up a hand to halt Lucas and Isaac so the crunch of their footsteps in the brittle winter grass wouldn't interfere with the sound. Sooner heard it, too, and Tyler knelt quickly to seize a fistful of the thick cinnamon-colored ruff around the dog's neck. There was no sense letting him hurtle recklessly down the hill to investigate before the cause of the sound was known.

Tyler listened again. It was a peculiar, honking racket, and it struck him as an animal's cry of pain or a plea for help.

"I know that holler right well!" Isaac exclaimed. "That be Patches—an' no respectable mule raise such a ruckus just to exercise his tonsils! You got any wild pigs hereabouts? Maybe one got into his pen and—"

The sound commenced again, and before Tyler could stop him, Sooner tore himself free and streaked like a flaming arrow down the slope toward the cow shed. It was true sometimes a wild boar did come nosing around and could be mighty pugnacious—but it was a much greater danger to a dog than a mule. His heart in his throat, Tyler leaped up and began to run.

Isaac flew down the hill, too, and with his long legs quickly outdistanced Tyler. Lucas, wiry and fleet-footed, was able to keep up with Isaac, and before he knew it, Tyler found himself lagging several yards behind. Panting, he rounded the corner of the cow shed, then stopped short as Lucas and Isaac plunged ahead.

Patches was backed into a corner of the pen, his eyes white-ringed with alarm. For a split second, Tyler almost laughed out loud. The old boy was even wider awake than he'd been when Lucas hustled him down the road at such a lively clip. But it was no wild pig that had Patches's attention. Any temptation to be amused evaporated the moment Tyler saw why the mule was making such a fuss.

Two men stood in front of him, one with a rope and halter in his hand. Their clothes were ragged. The hats clamped on their heads were soiled and greasy. There was a pistol strapped to the hip of the tall man who was about to drop the halter over Patches's head.

Scalawags!

Usually Patches was as docile as a kitten or just plain too sleepy to care what anyone did to him. Today, however, he must have sensed something about the two strangers that set him on edge, because each time the one stranger tried to pass the halter over his ears, the mule threw up his head and uttered another loud honk.

Sooner charged into the pen before Lucas or Isaac did. Tyler watched with hammering heart as the white-chested dog flew at both men from behind. His teeth were bared and his ears were laid as flat as an angry bob-cat's to his head.

Tyler remembered how Bigger flew at the man in the main street of McMinnville. He'd paid with his life that day, and Tyler shuddered when he saw Sooner sink his teeth smack into the scrawny buttocks of the man with the pistol. The fellow dropped the halter with a yelp and clutched at his rump with both hands.

The second man, much shorter than his companion, swung out with a heavy boot and nailed Sooner square in the ribs. It was Sooner's turn to yelp with pain, and he slunk warily out of range of the boot, his cool blue eye casting about for a fresh advantage, the brown one blazing with indignation.

Both men whirled as Isaac and Lucas burst into the pen. Tyler dropped low into the weeds at the corner of the shed, wondering if he had time to sneak up to the house and grab the Hawken from behind the door of Mama's room. He was just about to crawl away, then had to grind his fist against his teeth to choke off a groan of disappointment.

The second man reached for what looked like a stick leaning against the side of the pen. Lordy, lordy; it wasn't a stick! It was the Hawken. . . .

In a flash, Tyler understood what must have happened. While he and Lucas and Isaac had been putting Papa to rest at the top of the hill, the thieves had come up the road and found the cabin empty. Thinking its occupants were gone temporarily, they'd quickly ransacked it, taking anything of value they could lay their hands on. Tyler spied a mound of stuff the men had piled up nearby—Mama's favorite cooking pot, all the warm quilts, Papa's old coat with the buffalo-hair collar. The thieving rascals even had Calico and her calf tied up, ready to be led away. Not satisfied with their haul, now they aimed to take Patches, too.

The man with the pistol grabbed Lucas's arm and twisted it high up behind his back. Tyler heard his brother grunt with pain, and his heart swelled with pride when Lucas gritted his teeth and refused to cry out.

"Behave yourself, sonny!" the man barked. "An' you, boy," he snapped, turning to Isaac. "Get over there next to the fence with this little varmint. Don't either one of you move a hair." Isaac did exactly as he was told. He might brag about being a freedman, but Tyler knew he was accustomed to obeying orders whenever a white man yelled at him. That long red scar on his cheek was proof of what happened if he didn't.

No one looked in his direction, and Tyler realized neither of the scalawags had spotted him yet. He flattened himself deeper into the weeds. He saw Sooner cowering against the fence, tail tucked between his legs, and clucked softly to attract his attention. As the second man gave Lucas a hard shove with the butt of the Hawken, Sooner began to inch toward Tyler's hiding place.

"Say, Walt, what's that dawg doin'?" the tall man yelled when he spied Sooner slinking off. Tyler bit his lip. Maybe he'd made a terrible mistake trying to call Sooner to his side. What if the man pulled out his pistol and blew Sooner to kingdom come?

"Aw, he's yella, can't you see? Lookit his belly hug the ground! I scared the living b'jeezus outta him with that kick in the slats," the man named Walt snickered. "Quit worrying about the mutt! Just throw a halter on that fool mule so we can git movin' before anyone else shows up around here."

Behind the shed, Tyler pressed his hand over Sooner's white bib. Underneath, he could feel the dog's heart hammer as hard as his own. It was exactly like the old woman had told him when he'd gone looking for Papa: "Since the war ended, folks say the country's being over-run by thieves. Scalawags is what they're calling 'em." She said they stole horses, cattle, food, money—anything that was light and loose, then wandered on to the next place to do the same thing all over again.

"Where's the menfolk on this place?" the tall man demanded of Lucas. The question caused the color to drain out of Lucas's face, and when he didn't answer right away, the man rapped him smartly alongside the head with the barrel of the pistol. A streak of bright blood spurted from the scratch he left on Lucas's temple.

Suddenly, a gleam appeared in the man's eye. "Why, there ain't no men here, is there?" he taunted when Lucas didn't speak up. A slow grin of spread across the stranger's face. "Ain't you even got a mama, sonny? A mama that can put on a meal for us?"

"Don't have one," Tyler heard Lucas mumble. Tyler smiled grimly. *Bless you, Lucas!* he said silently. That was a smart answer and suddenly gave Tyler an idea.

If the thieves believed they were dealing only with three boys, it might make them careless. Then, if a way could be found to distract the scalawags and get them at a disadvantage, maybe the tables could be turned on them. A plan swiftly took shape in Tyler's head.

He rose quickly out of the weeds and stepped from behind the shed.

"That's right," he called, striding boldly forward. "Ain't nobody here but us boys." The man with the pistol whirled and aimed straight at Tyler's heart so quick it made him suck in his breath with terror.

"It's just like Lucas said," he rattled on in a shaky voice. "Ain't nobody here but my brother and me and Isaac. Papa's dead in the war. Mama passed on from some kind of fever. Fact is, we just buried her up there on the hill." He jerked his thumb in the direction from which they'd just come.

Walt, the shorter of the two men, smirked. "All alone, eh?" He winked at his companion. "In that case, sounds to me like this might be a good place for me an' Miller to settle down for a spell." He glanced at the garden. "Looks like your ma probably put some food by before the Lord called her home. Reckon that means you could rustle up a meal for us, sonny."

Tyler nodded; his plan was working better than he'd hoped.

Walt gestured impatiently with the barrel of the Hawken. "Get on up to the cabin, hear? We ain't had decent food in too long to even mention." Then he glanced at Lucas and Isaac.

"Miller, tie them boys up. Keepin' an eye on three young bucks all at the same time is two too many." Tyler watched as Miller looped the rope that had been intended for Patches around Isaac and Lucas. He tied them back to back, then cinched the end of the rope around one of the posts in the cow pen and gave it a sharp tug.

"Didn't you hear me, sonny? You get on up to the house," Walt hollered irritably when he noticed Tyler hadn't budged.

"Don't worry," Tyler hissed as he stumbled past Lucas and Isaac. "I got a plan."

"Better be a good one—or we be three dead boys!" Isaac whispered in return.

In the kitchen, Tyler set out two plates and got some cold roast venison Mama had left on a high shelf on the porch where it would keep cool and animals wouldn't get it. When the two thieves plunked themselves down at the table as if they owned the place,

Tyler busied himself stoking up the woodstove.

"Got a whole cellar full of taters and rooty-beggars out back," he said. "While I get this stove goin', you can fetch whatever you want." He settled the stove lids in place. "Uh, almost forgot. Papa kept some whiskey out there, too," he added. "It's way toward the back, behind that big mound of carrots."

He watched from the corner of his eye as the two men exchanged delighted glances. "Whiskey! Say, Miller, it's been a while since you and me had a good snort! I'll go get it," Walt declared.

"Make sure you don't drink it all before you get it back here," Tyler murmured slyly. The man named Miller frowned. "The kid's got a point, Walt. You always was thirstier'n a goat! Maybe I'll just go with you to make sure you don't chug-a-lug the whole danged bottle before I get a drop." He reached across the table and picked up the Hawken.

Doggone it! Tyler groaned silently. That wasn't part of the plan. Miller was supposed to walk out and leave the Hawken behind!

"Just to be on the safe side, sonny, you come along with us," Miller ordered. "That way, me and Walt here will be sure you won't get into mischief. Never mind the stove; it'll be all right till we get back."

"But I was goin' to fix you some—"

"You can fix it later," Miller barked.

Tyler realized his scheme was falling apart so fast he couldn't figure out a way to fix it. He hurried out the door as he was told, the barrel of the Hawken jabbed sharply against his backbone. Neither of the men saw Sooner crouched as flat as a badger under the porch. As they all trekked around the corner of the cabin, Tyler saw Sooner creep out from his hiding place and follow, his belly to the ground as before. It occurred to him that maybe Sooner had a plan of his own.

Walt wasted no time getting the cellar open. "Whoa, there! Wait for me," Miller called, and poked Tyler again. "You get in there, too, sonny. That way, I'll know exactly where you're at."

Tyler decided there was only one thing left to try. Within five feet of the cellar door he pretended to stub his toe. He sprawled headlong on the ground and let out a yowl. "Ooowww!" he squawked as if in terrible pain. "My ankle! I think it's broke—eeeooowww!"

"Stupid, clumsy brat!" Miller snapped. He reached down, grabbed Tyler by the arm, and jerked him upright. "Broke your ankle? What kind of fool you take me for! You think I don't know every trick in the book? That bird-with-the-broken-wing trick is so old it's got gray hair!"

Miller leaned so close Tyler could feel the man's breath on his cheek. His eyes were narrow and savage, and there was no hint of ordinary human pity in them. Tyler reminded himself that this was the same man who'd drawn blood from Lucas. "You try to run another whizzer on me, boy," Miller warned, "and you won't be long for this world!" Then the scalawag spied Sooner sneaking along behind.

"Say! Ain't that the mutt that bit me? Why, I got half a notion to pay him back right now!" He lifted the Hawken and prepared to sight down its barrel. "I'll teach the stupid pooch some manners, all right! Might as well blow his head off while I'm at it—"

Tyler shuddered. It would be a horrible replay of Bigger's death in McMinnville. Desperately, he waved Sooner back, relieved when the dog halted and flattened himself into the grass again. "Leave 'im be, mister," Tyler muttered. "I'll do whatever you say."

Miller lowered the Hawken with a snort of disgust. "An' what I say is git your rear end into that root cellar and be quick about it!"

Tyler felt the rifle muzzle in his ribs and stumbled obediently into the cool, musty darkness of the cellar. *Why had he imagined he could outwit men like these?* Who could tell what sort of crimes they'd already committed . . . a boy's life or a dog's life meant nothing to them.

Walt had already made his way past the potatoes, had gotten down on his hands and knees, and was crawling between the mound of carrots on one side and one of rutabagas on the other. "Step away from the doorway!" Walt yelled over his shoulder. "It's blacker'n midnight back here and I need all the light I can get to find that doggone whiskey!"

"It's stashed way to the back, on account of Mama didn't hold with liquor," Tyler said weakly, hoping to get Walt as far from Miller as possible. "Bottle must be almost full, seeing as how nobody's touched it since Papa went off to catch up with General Shelby."

When Miller stepped aside to let in more light, Tyler reached swiftly toward the sand-covered mountain of potatoes. He snatched up two and pitched the first one at Miller as hard as he could. The spud caught the scalawag square between the eyes, making a sound like a melon smashed against a stone. He threw the second one even harder and nailed Miller smack on the nose.

The scalawag dropped the Hawken and doubled over, one hand over his nose, which immediately spurted blood. "Why, you rotten little son of a—"

Tyler considered making a grab for the rifle. No, it was too risky; it would bring him within an arm's length of Miller. Instead, he darted through the open door. He grabbed the stout two-inch-thick wooden bar that Papa had made to fit into a pair of brackets on either side of the heavy plank door. He slammed the door shut and dropped the bar into place just as Miller heaved his weight against it from the other side.

No matter how hard the two thieves hurled themselves against it, however, Tyler knew the door would never give way. There was no need to worry about them crawling out a window, either, because there wasn't one in the root cellar. Tyler recalled he'd been careful to remove the shovel last fall when he carried in the last load of sand, so there was no way for them to dig their way out. If they tried to scratch their way to freedom with their bare hands, it'd take them a month of Sundays.

Tyler ran back to the pen and untied Lucas and Isaac. "Did you kill 'em?" Lucas wanted to know as Tyler struggled with the rope.

"I don't aim to kill anybody if I can help it," Tyler said. "I got those fellas locked up in the root cellar. I told 'em there was whiskey in there."

Isaac slapped his knee softly. "You think quick, Ty! Whiskey—the one thing such fellas couldn't turn down."

"What about their guns?" Lucas demanded.

Tyler regretted that he asked. "They've still got 'em," he admitted.

"And *we* still got nothing!" Lucas exclaimed.

Tyler frowned. "We don't have to worry about that, at least not right away. We can keep those fellas in the cellar until we figure out what to do next. They won't die in there, not for a while anyway. They've even got something to eat—if they don't mind eating sandy carrots or gritty spuds, that is."

"They got something to drink, too," Lucas reminded

him. "That whiskey you told 'em about."

Tyler eeked out a thin smile. "They'll look for it a long time. Ain't no such thing in there. You know how Mama felt about spirits."

The scalawags yelled and pounded on the door for most of the afternoon. The threats they made were colorful and caused Lucas and Isaac to roll their eyes in mock alarm.

"Soon as we get outta here we'll boil you in oil, boy!"

"Sonny, we'll whup your backside till it's raw!"

"You miserable little varmint, you'll get slapped silly for lyin' to us about that whiskey!"

Tyler and Lucas grinned and nudged each other, but after a few more threats, Isaac ceased to be amused. "We just better hope they never get loose," he warned. He touched the scar on his cheek. "A white man gits mad like that—well, you don't want to be near him when he does."

"We'll just try to get through today and tomorrow," Tyler admitted, and felt his bowels knot up with anxiety. "Let's see. Mama left this morning, and the funeral will probably be tomorrow. Oat will most likely have her back by suppertime. By then, maybe we can figure something out." He studied Lucas and Isaac. "Tonight we'll take turns keeping watch out here, to make sure we don't get taken by surprise again."

But when nighttime came, Lucas's nerves wouldn't handle doing sentry duty alone. Tyler and Isaac gathered up the quilts Walt and Miller had been about to steal, and they all trekked outside to stay together beside the root cellar. While Lucas and Isaac dozed, Tyler took his turn keeping watch.

At last, no sounds came from inside the cellar. The scalawags had worn themselves out yelling and beating on the door. The threats they'd hurled all afternoon had grown weaker and less colorful. They must have finally dropped off to sleep themselves.

Tyler sat cross-legged, then drew his quilt around his shoulders to make a tent. Sooner whined softly, but made no move to crawl into the tent himself. Tyler was pretty sure he knew what made him keep his distance.

"You feel bad on account of you couldn't figure out what to do about those scalawags, right?" Sooner whined apologetically and rested his head on his paws. Tyler opened the quilt and beckoned the dog inside.

"It's all right, Sooner," he soothed. "You did the best you could, just like I did. Main thing is, neither one of us got killed." Sooner snuggled gratefully into the nest made by Tyler's crossed legs and folded his plumy tail across his nose.

Overhead, the sky was dense with stars. It had been an old habit to pray that Papa looked up at the same moon and stars that he saw himself.

"Don't have to wonder where Papa's at anymore," Tyler said with a sigh, grateful for Sooner's weight and warmth against his own body. He glanced up the hillside, burnished with star shine. Because of what he and Lucas and Isaac had done this morning, Papa's spirit was at ease for all eternity under the same sky that arched over Sweet Creek.

Chapter Eleven

As dawn turned the horizon pink, the boys crawled out of their quilts. They stretched, then listened for sounds of life from the prisoners. Nothing could be heard from inside the cellar. Finally, Tyler laid his ear against the door. He stepped back with a frown. "I don't hear a thing," he said.

"Maybe they died during the night," Lucas whispered.

"Or maybe they found a way out," Isaac countered, and cast a fearful glance over his shoulder.

"Not a chance," Tyler scoffed. "Look—nothing's been disturbed—not the door, not the dirt over top of the cellar, nary a thing. Besides, I was awake most of the night."

But what if Lucas was right, that somehow the men had perished in the cool, inky blackness on the other side of the door? The possibility that Walt and Miller were lying in there, lifeless, their hands crossed prayerfully on their chests, made Tyler shiver. On the other hand, they might only be asleep. He stepped up to the door again and tapped politely.

There was a rustle and a groan from the other side. "'Bout time you got back here, sonny!" came a weary cry even before the sound of his knock had died away. "Now you let us outta here this minute, hear?" It was the tall man's voice, and though he sounded tired, he was also plainly furious.

"Nossir, Mr. Miller, I can't do that," Tyler apologized, glad the door was as stout as it was because Miller began to hammer his fists on it with almost as much energy as he had the day before. "As long as you're in there, us boys don't have to worry about you and Walt taking up your mean, thievin' habits again."

A muffled conference took place on the opposite side of the door, which meant Walt was quite alive, too. "But you can't leave us in here, boy," Walt pleaded in a more conciliatory fashion. "We got no water, son, nothin' at all to drink." His voice was raspy, as if his throat was as scratchy as the sand covering the piles of vegetables.

"You fibbed to us about there bein' whiskey in here, and you know the Lord don't hold with lyin'," Walt croaked. "A man could die in this place. You wouldn't want that on your conscience, would you?"

Tyler snorted. Who was *he* to talk about the Lord, much less anybody's conscience?

"You fellas have still got weapons, and us boys don't have anything to defend ourselves with," Tyler pointed out. "Long as you've got our rifle and Mr. Miller has his pistol, ain't no way we can trust you." He paused. "We're goin' off to fix ourselves some breakfast now, but we'll be back every couple hours to check up on you."

"Breakfast!" Miller screeched with outrage. "Why, you little weasel! When I get my hands on—"

"No, no, sonny! Hang on there a minute!" Walt interrupted. "We'll make you a deal!" He began to claw frantically at his side of the door. Tyler imagined Walt's fingernails shredding on those rough boards; even now, maybe he was leaving drops of blood on the wood.

"This dark is making me crazy! And I'm terrible thirsty . . . you gotta let me out, son!"

But Tyler retreated, beckoning Lucas and Isaac to follow, and when they got back to the cabin, he started a fire. As water heated for a potful of mush, he outlined the dilemma as he saw it. "Those fellas might be thirsty and hungry, but they're still not near weak enough for us to take a chance on turning 'em loose." Isaac nodded vigorously in agreement.

"That means we'll have to wait till they get so feeble they'll do most anything we ask just for a sip of water," Tyler went on. "Otherwise, first thing they'll want to do when they set foot outside that cellar is even the score with us. Might start blazing away with one of those guns and we'd end up worse off than we were in the beginning."

"But what if Mama gets home before they're ready to give up?" Lucas asked.

"If she does, she does," Tyler muttered.

"Maybe you should try to call on Mr. Snepp for help," Isaac suggested.

"He's burying his wife," Tyler reminded him. "Not a good time to bust in on the man, I'd say."

"Then maybe we ought to try to get help from McMinnville!" Lucas exclaimed.

"On foot? It'd take most of a day—because I'm pretty sure Patches couldn't make such a long trip," Tyler pointed out. "Anyway, which one of us would go? Isaac is a stranger in these parts; *you* want to go alone, Lucas?" The suggestion made Lucas turn pale.

"Means we'd better stick together right here. Our best bet is to keep those men prisoners till we're sure they're too faint to raise a pinkie against us."

Tyler remembered something he'd heard Mr. Blackburn say in class. A person could live for many days without food, but only a short time without water. If that was so, it might take only a few more hours for the prisoners to agree to any condition that would allow them to quench their thirst.

"But how'll we know for sure when they're feeble enough?" Isaac asked dubiously. "We be on the outside of that door. They be on the inside. Means we can't *see* 'em—so how'll we be sure what kind of shape they're truly in?"

Tyler frowned. "They've been in there since yesterday noon. Soon it'll be twenty-four hours." It was hard to know what Mr. Blackburn meant when he said "a short time"; did it mean two days or a week, or what? Tyler glanced at the clock Mama kept on a shelf near the door. "By tonight, there'll be nothing on their minds except a drink of cool, clear water. The next day, they'll be even more desperate. All we got to do is wait."

Meantime, there was milking to be done, Patches to be exercised, and dozens of small chores tended to so the place would look tidy when Mama got home—partly to please her, partly to impress Oat.

At noon the voices of the scalawags were weaker, but their threats turned meaner. The boys listened as Miller and Walt raged about beating their captors within an inch of their lives. About slapping them so hard their teeth would fall out of their heads. About hanging them by their thumbs from the oak tree near the porch. They even mentioned the word *kill*. Such threats made Isaac shudder, and Tyler saw him lay his hand over the scar on his cheek each time the scalawags conjured up a new punishment.

By nightfall, however, the captives' voices were much

fainter. There were no more threats. Walt's voice had a thin, hopeless sound in it. Only Miller was still strong enough to turn the air blue with an occasional angry curse. All day long, Tyler had listened for the sound of wagon wheels across the bridge, but by bedtime none had been heard.

"You boys go on upstairs," he told Isaac and Lucas after supper. "Just to be on the safe side, Sooner and me will keep watch out yonder." He actually didn't mind doing sentry duty again. In a way, it made him think about when he'd traveled all the way to Texas by himself.

He looped an arm around Sooner's neck as once he'd looped it around Bigger's. Over the last few weeks, Sooner had lost the bumbling, lanky look of a pup. His neck was getting thick and sturdy; his shoulders had filled out, his chest was deeper. Last night Tyler had passed the time thinking about Papa; tonight, looking into Sooner's star-filled pale blue eye, he told him stories about *his* father.

"Bigger was something else," he began. "You would've been proud of your papa, too, Sooner." In a way, Tyler knew he was talking about himself. It was hard not to be proud of Papa for sticking with a cause he believed in.

At noon on the third day, Sooner began to bark before the Snepps' wagon set a wheel on the bridge, and for once Tyler didn't mind eyeballing Oat again. Except that it wasn't Oat who sat on the left side of the wagon bench, Mama on the far side, Rosa Lee nestled snugly in between. It was Mr. Snepp himself. He was dressed somberly in his black funeral suit, his high white shirt collar starched so stiff it drew a red mark under his chin like a hangman's noose.

Mr. Snepp clambered down from the wagon, then

lifted Rosa Lee down as if she were made of china and might break if not handled properly. Tyler smiled. Mr. Snepp clearly didn't know what kind of girl Rosa Lee was—the kind who was as quick to throw a punch as Lucas! But Rosa Lee surprised Tyler; she looked pleased at being treated so politely and shyly murmured, "Thank you," like a regular girl.

Then Mr. Snepp went around to the other side of the wagon, held out his hand, and helped Mama alight, too. Well, now. Tyler felt his jaw muscles tighten with annoyance. Mama was a grown woman who'd gotten into and out of many a wagon; she could do it perfectly well on her own.

"You come right inside, Elway," Mama invited, "and rest a bit before you head for home." She'd gone to help bury Mr. Snepp's wife; did that somehow mean she could call him Elway now? Poor Mrs. Snepp was hardly cool in her grave yet. Tyler frowned and stuck his fists deep into his pockets.

"Boys, do you have a fire going, so I can make a bit of tea for our guest?" Suddenly, Mr. Snepp wasn't even regular company—he was a guest!

"Yes, Mama, we do." Tyler wasn't sure just how or when to explain about the captives in the root cellar. Maybe it would be best to wait till Mr. Snepp was gone; however, it was a temptation to let Elway Snepp know that Mama's sons weren't ordinary boys. They could be counted on to look after their mother just fine, thank you!

Mama was delighted to find the kitchen so tidy and made quite a fuss of serving Elway Snepp tea in the only nice china cup she owned. "Maybe you'll stay long enough for me to put a meal on for you," she suggested. Tyler gritted his teeth. Lordy, hadn't she already done enough for Mr. Snepp?

"The boys and I have been lucky this year," she chattered on. Tyler was surprised; usually she was on the quiet side. "Tyler got us some venison awhile back, and we have lots of things put down in our root cellar."

Tyler saw Lucas and Isaac roll their eyes toward the ceiling beams the minute the word *cellar* was mentioned. "Mama, we got something else in that cellar now!" Lucas blurted. Shoot! The cat was out of the bag now.

"Whatever are you talking about, Lucas?" Mama asked as she laid out some buttered bread for Mr. Snepp to eat with his tea. She didn't sound too concerned about the answer.

"We got two critters locked up in there," Tyler said bluntly in a too-loud voice.

"You've got *what* in there?" Ah, now she was paying attention! "What do you mean, 'two critters'? Ones that'll eat up all the provisions we worked so hard to put by? Goodness, Tyler, whatever were you boys thinking of?"

"We locked two men up in there, Mama. Fellas who figured to clean us out of everything they could pack off—all our quilts and your cook pots, Calico and her calf, Patches, Papa's old Hawken rifle—everything they could carry away."

Mama laid her hand over her heart as if she felt some sort of spell coming on. Rosa Lee completely forgot she was a piece of breakable china. "There's two men in our root cellar?" she screeched, and snatched a piece of kindling out of the wood-box to bludgeon them with. Mr. Snepp, who had listened silently, spoke up in his soft bank clerk's voice.

"Umm. Sounds like some scalawags paid you a visit while your mama was gone," he said, and leaned forward to rest his freckled hands squarely on his knees.

Tyler nodded. "Yessir, that's exactly what we figured.

Trouble is, we managed to get 'em into the cellar all right, but now I can't figure out how to let 'em out." Tyler remembered how soft Mr. Snepp's handshake had been but noticed now that he didn't seem fearful to hear scalawags were nearby or excuse himself hastily, saying he'd better head for home.

"Those fellas have been in there two whole days now. They're getting pretty weak on account of they haven't had any water or hardly anything to eat except some sandy carrots or gritty spuds," Tyler explained. "The problem is, one of 'em has a pistol and the other one's got our Hawken."

Mr. Snepp tapped his knees. "Maybe I can help you boys out," he murmured. "I've got my Winchester under the bench of my wagon," he said. "Never go anywhere without it." A Winchester? But that's what Papa had! Somehow, Mr. Snepp didn't seem like the sort who'd own such a weapon. Elway Snepp squinted thoughtfully as he drummed a light tattoo on his knees.

"Unless I miss my guess, your root cellar is built pretty much like ours. Back into the hillside, am I right?"

Tyler nodded.

"Means if a man with a good rifle took a mind to, he could stand overhead, right above the door, and draw a bead on whoever came out below."

Tyler saw Lucas's and Isaac's eyes widen in anticipation of a lively showdown. "We'll tell those fellas we've got arms of our own and offer to let them walk out with their hands up," Mr. Snepp went on in his steady, prudent way. "I'll stand guard above, while all of you"—he glanced first at Rosa Lee, then his gaze lingered briefly on Mama—"while you boys and the ladies stand aside, out of harm's way."

"What if those men come out with their weapons

blazing?" Lucas demanded. He seemed bent on enjoying some kind of gunfire.

Elway Snepp seemed just as bent on preventing it. "I'll order those chaps to throw their guns out first. If they refuse, why, then I might just have to shoot them the minute they step through the doorway. Shooting any man in the back is not a noble prospect, mind you, and not a deed I'd be proud to commit." Tyler was astonished. Elway Snepp—red hair, freckles, soft handshake, and all—was the kind of man who was willing to do what needed to be done. Quietly, without fanfare.

"Most likely, no shooting will be necessary," Mr. Snepp went on. "You say those fellas have been holed up in the dark for two days? In that case, their eyes won't adjust real quick to bright light. It's bright today—one of the sunniest days we've had for a week—so even if they want to use their weapons they'll be at a serious disadvantage."

Mr. Snepp tapped his knees again and seemed pleased. "To put it another way, boys, *we* hold the best cards in this game."

Lucas grinned, impressed by Elway Snepp's vow to shoot the scalawags if necessary. Tyler hated to admit it, but he was sort of impressed himself.

Mr. Snepp peeled off his coat and stripped the starched collar from his neck. "Ma'am, you stay indoors with Rosa Lee," he told Mama gently. "Your boys and I will take care of these rascals." For once, Rosa Lee didn't stick out her lip or get set to have a hissy-fit.

Tyler heard Lucas whisper to Isaac, "And if those men don't do just like Mr. Snepp says—*bam!*—he'll blast 'em so they stay blasted!"

"Let's hope it doesn't come to that," Tyler cautioned. He remembered too well how he felt about the young buck. How its blood had drained away in a scarlet trail in the snow as he and Lucas had dragged the carcass home. Even though he hated what the scalawags had tried to do, he didn't relish seeing them get killed unless there was no other way to handle them.

Not a sound emanated from the root cellar when they went out to stand in front of the plank door. Again, Tyler knocked politely. From inside came a cry so feeble it sounded like the mewing of a sick cat.

"Is that you, boy?" Miller croaked. He'd been the meanest of the pair; now he sounded almost harmless. "You better let us outta here. . . . We're on the verge of perishing . . . ain't got much strength left. Boy . . . you still there?"

"Yessir, I'm still here," Tyler answered. "And I got a bucketful of nice cool springwater waiting for you. I got to warn you, though, we boys got some help now." Elway Snepp nodded, then stepped nimbly to the top of the cellar, the blue barrel of his Winchester winking in the sunshine.

There was a moment of silence inside. "Help? What kinda help do you mean?" Was it his imagination, Tyler wondered, or did Miller suddenly sound crafty? "You claimed all your kin were dead, son." As desperate as he was, Tyler detected a thin edge of slyness in Miller's reminder. He might be weak, but he still was clever.

"Our neighbor, Mr. Elway Snepp, has come by to help us out, Mr. Miller. He's got himself a fine rifle, one of them fancy repeating kind that fires off several rounds real quick. Have you heard about them new Winchesters, Mr. Miller?"

"B'leeve I have, son." The craftiness leaked out of Miller's voice.

"Well, sir, I'm goin' to take the bar off this door. Mr.

Snepp will be standing where you can't see him," Tyler explained. "I'll step aside, then you fellas throw your weapons out. Come out one at a time, your hands in the air. If you don't, remember Mr. Snepp's got the advantage because you don't know where he's at. Mind you, he'll shoot, no questions asked."

Again, there was silence on the opposite side of the door. "Son, I b'leeve you're running a whizzer on me again," Miller said coldly. "You told us there was whiskey in his cellar—but you lied! Now you're tellin' me there's a man with a Winchester out there—"

Tyler glanced quickly at Mr. Snepp, who smiled thinly. "The boy's not lying, gentlemen," Mr. Snepp called out in a steady voice. "Let me add that I rarely miss what I aim at, either." He lifted the muzzle of his Winchester skyward and fired it into the air, causing blue jays to explode from the oak tree in front of the cabin. Lucas and Isaac grinned from ear to ear; even Tyler felt a grudging admiration for Mr. Snepp's coolness.

"Whatever you say," came Walt's faint cry. "Anything . . . for a drink . . . of water . . ."

"Mr. Miller?" Tyler asked. "Do you believe me now?"

It took Miller a moment to answer. When he did, it seemed to Tyler that all the fight had drained out of him. "Reckon you're one up on us, boy," he admitted.

Tyler waved Lucas to one side and Isaac to the other. Lucas knelt and took hold of Sooner by the ruff of the neck to keep him from attacking either of the prisoners. Then Tyler stepped forward, quickly lifted the bolt out of its twin brackets, and jumped aside himself. He left the water bucket in full view, ten feet from the cellar entrance, to force the scalawags to walk clear of the door.

The door swung slowly open of its own weight.

Sooner gave a low, throaty growl and once again flattened himself like a badger, ready to spring if given half a chance.

First, the Hawken came sailing through the doorway. Miller's pistol followed a moment later. Miller himself, even scrawnier than he'd been before, staggered out into the bright sunshine. He held his hands over his eyes to shield them from the noonday glare. Walt didn't have strength enough to stand up. Instead, he crawled out on his hands and knees, head hanging like a whipped dog's, eyes squinched shut against the light. He collapsed face-down on the ground only four feet from the bucket, too weak to move another inch.

"Now you fellas stay right where you're at," Elway Snepp called from his post atop the cellar. "Tyler, you pick up the Hawken; you, Lucas, grab that pistol." Then Mr. Snepp came down and nudged Walt gently with the point of his Winchester. "On your feet, my friend." Walt struggled to get up, then Mr. Snepp urged the thieves forward with another poke from his rifle.

"Water," Walt croaked. "You promised us water . . ." Tyler held out a dipperful, and Walt gulped it down so eagerly it spilled down his chin and onto his front, which was covered with sand from the piles inside the cellar.

"What'll we do with 'em now?" Lucas wanted to know.

"While I keep my rifle on 'em, you boys tie these chaps up real good," Mr. Snepp directed. "Then we'll load 'em into my wagon like a couple sacks of flour. I'll take them over to McMinnville. It's closer than New Hope, and besides they got a U.S. marshal there who'll know what to do with the likes of these two."

"That's a far trip, and you haven't had a bite to eat," Mama said, who had hurried outside with Rosa Lee once the men had surrendered. "Maybe you ought to stay over and leave in the morning."

"I'd just as soon hustle along, ma'am," Mr. Snepp replied. "Oat won't worry if I'm gone only overnight, but I'm loathe to leave my boys to themselves longer than that"—He hesitated a moment—"considering they so recently lost their mama. It'd help if Tyler and Lucas could come along to lend me a hand, though, if that's agreeable to you."

Lucas's black eyes gleamed with delight, and Tyler knew he was ready to climb onto the wagon without waiting for a second invitation. "Take Lucas and Isaac with you, Mr. Snepp," Tyler said. "They'll be all the help you need. Sooner and me will stay behind to make sure Mama and Rosa Lee are looked after in case there's any other trouble."

The swift glance Lucas gave him almost made the whole ordeal worthwhile. "I'm the one who went away last time; now it's your turn," Tyler said. He turned to Isaac. "You come on back, Isaac—unless you got a mind to be headed elsewhere."

"Nossir, I'll be back with Lucas," Isaac promised. "Remember, we got them crops to put in."

"Ah, speaking of which," Mr. Snepp said, smiling widely for the first time since he'd arrived, "when I come back maybe we can talk about hemp."

Chapter Twelve

IT SEEMED STRANGE to have only three around the supper table that evening, and Tyler said so. "Strange to you, but not to us," Mama corrected, lifting an eyebrow. "After all, this is the way it was the whole long time you were gone to Texas. It was just Lucas and Rosa Lee and me for every meal."

This time it was Lucas who was absent, though, and Tyler realized it gave him the perfect chance to let Mama know how they'd committed Papa's spirit to the top of the hill. If his brother had been sitting right across the table, Tyler knew he'd have to pick his words carefully. For Lucas, mentioning the funeral again so soon would be as painful as picking at a fresh scab.

"Why, I think that was a fine thing to do and would please your papa," Mama said when Tyler finished telling her what they'd done while she was taking part in a real funeral over at the Snepp place. She seemed especially grateful to hear about Isaac's song and to know it fit Papa so well. "Tomorrow, you can take Rosa Lee and me up there so we can pay our respects, too," she suggested. Her invitation came as a relief; Tyler hadn't been sure she'd want to share the experience.

When they set out after breakfast the next day, Sooner gamboling in front of them as if he knew exactly where they were headed, Tyler was surprised that Mama didn't talk about Papa. Instead, she talked about what had gone on at the Snepps', where an honest-to-goodness service had been held, with Reverend Tucker from McMinnville reading from the Bible and neighbors gathered around to pay their final respects.

"It was hard for all the Snepps," Mama explained, "especially for the smaller children." She glanced out over the familiar countryside, brushed a stray lock of hair from her cheek, and seemed lost in her own thoughts. "But the truth is, sometimes death can be a blessing, Ty. As when a person is destined never to get well, which poor Lottie Snepp surely was not."

Tyler felt his heart shrivel to the size of a walnut to think she felt it was a blessing that Isaac brought the news about Papa. He wanted to believe Papa would be in her thoughts forever, just as she'd been in his as he lay dying down there on the coast of Brazil.

"Of course, it wasn't the same thing with your papa," Mama went on, reflecting on the difference before Tyler could speak up himself. "Your papa wasn't laid low by a terrible sickness that wore him down to skin and bones. No, son, your papa was busy adventuring. Doing what he believed he had to do, right to the very end. You might say when death came for John Bohannon, it came partly at his invitation."

Ahead, Sooner bounded up the slope, lured by the bobbing white tail of a rabbit. Surely Mama was mistaken! Tyler didn't want to think it was Papa's fault that he'd died. To change the subject, he wondered aloud, "Umm— how is Oat getting along?" With his mother gone, there'd be no one to tell him how to make bread or fix stew or what to do when one of his little brothers was ailing.

"He's a dutiful boy and will do his best," Mama said, smiling. "In a way, Oat is very much like you, Ty."

Tyler stared at her. "I don't think so!" he exclaimed indignantly. No way was he a high-and-mighty Mr. Know-It-All! No way was he a look-down-his-nose sort of person!

"You had to be the man of the house on this side of Sweet Creek," Mama explained, "and you could say Oat had to be the lady of the house on the other side while his poor mama did her dying." Tyler was relieved when they arrived at the top of the hill because the conversation certainly hadn't been the kind he'd hoped they'd have. He hoisted Rosa Lee up in his arms so she could look over the valley below, could see the bridge clearly and how Sweet Creek wended its way south.

"But where is Papa?" Rosa Lee wanted to know. "You said you boys buried him up here, Ty, only I don't see a grave."

Tyler saw a shadow in his sister's dark eyes he'd never seen before. Ah. Having been a witness to Mrs. Snepp's burial, she'd learned something about death she'd never known before. Now she knew a person was put in a pine box and was laid to rest in the earth, then covered up to await the coming of Judgment Day. Never again would *death* be just a word to Rosa Lee.

"It was Papa's spirit we committed to this place," Tyler told her, "on account of we didn't have his body to bury. But he's here just the same, Rosa Lee. He's in the air, in the way the birds sing, in the way the sun comes up over the crest of the hill and how it sets over yonder along the ridge. Ain't that so, Mama?"

"Indeed it is," Mama assured Rosa Lee. "If your papa's spirit was going to return to anyplace at all, it would be here at home, to the place he loved best in all the world." She paused. "Even though he couldn't see fit to come back to it when he had the chance." Tyler wished she hadn't added that last remark. It brought another verdict down on Papa's head, same as that comment about him inviting death to his side.

Yet Mama had a point. Papa had pledged himself not to give up until those boys in blue had taken their licks and gone back North where they belonged. It was that old thing about dreams, how a person could cling to them so tightly, they actually kept him from being what he ought to be.

"Well, now let's go back and see if those scalawags created a big mess in our root cellar," Mama said briskly, as if she had finished any mourning she intended to do and was eager to take up ordinary life again. "If they did, Ty, we'll put it to right. Then you'll have to milk, and by evening, Elway might be back." She turned from the hilltop in a resolute way, her shoulders square. It seemed to Tyler there was nothing of a grieving widow in her posture.

He followed Mama silently down the hill. Worse, there was that name again. *Elway*. Spoken with a funny little inflection. There was a note—Tyler hated to imagine such a thing—of interest in it. As if Mama actually looked forward to seeing chipmunk-cheeked Mr. Snepp again.

That couldn't be, could it? The poor man had only been a widower for a few days. Tyler brushed his worry aside. Mama could likely never look at anyone again as she'd once looked at Black Jack Bohannon. When a person loved someone like Mama had loved Papa—had children with him and built a cabin and made plans for crops—after that, surely no other man would ever do.

* * *

When Elway Snepp returned earlier than expected that afternoon, it was plain that Lucas had never had as great an adventure. "We took those scalawags straight to the U.S. marshal's office, and he put handcuffs on them," he reported, his black eyes shining with satisfaction. "He said it was against the law to do what they'd been doin' and he'd see that they were held accountable. Then we went to the general store—and Mr. Snepp treated me and Isaac to some candy!"

"Candy!" Rosa Lee shrieked, forgetting she'd acted almost like a lady just a day ago. Tears welled up in her eyes and out came her famous lip. "Oh, I wish I coulda gone, too!" she wailed. She stamped both feet, then the tears began to flow in earnest.

"Now there, missy, do you think I would forget a pretty girl like you?" soothed Mr. Snepp as he knelt on one knee so his face was level with hers. He drew a small package from inside his black funeral coat. The gift was wrapped in shiny paper and tied with a piece of bright red string. Rosa Lee blinked her tears away and unwrapped it with trembly fingers. Inside was a small locket that opened on a hinge.

"Someday, when you have your picture taken, you'll be able to put it in this locket and keep it forever," Mr. Snepp said. For once, Rosa Lee was speechless.

"Do you have something to say to Mr. Snepp?" Mama prompted gently.

"Th-Thank you," Rosa Lee whispered, suddenly a lady again. Tyler realized he should be glad for his sister, not to mention for the candy Lucas and Isaac had enjoyed. Yet when he observed the smiling glance that Mama gave Mr. Snepp over Rosa's bowed head, he felt his own heart give an agonized thonk.

No! he objected silently. All right, so Mr. Snepp had

done them all a good turn by taking care of those scalawags—but now let him be on his way home where he belonged. "Oat's probably waiting on you," Tyler suggested politely, just in case Mr. Snepp had forgotten he had a family of his own that needed him even more than the Bohannons did.

"Indeed he is," Mr. Snepp agreed, "and I will be hurrying on in a moment. First, though, I have something for your mother."

Doggone, did the man have no shame? Tyler wondered bitterly. His poor wife hadn't even gotten used to being dead yet! However, what Elway Snepp placed on the table wasn't a package wrapped in fancy paper nor did it have shiny red string around it. It was a plain brown package of seed.

"Now your mama and you boys can plant yourselves some hemp as soon as it gets warm enough for you to work up the soil," he said, still smiling in that careful way he had. Tyler suspected he might grow to detest that small, cautious smile.

"Why, you remembered!" Mama exclaimed, her cheeks pink with delight. You'd think those seeds were made of solid gold, Tyler thought sourly. After her first burst of pleasure, though, Mama started to act all flustery.

"It'll be suppertime soon and and it's no trouble to make an extra place at the table—"

Hush, Mama! Tyler wanted to tell her. *Let the man go back to his own life.*

"No, ma'am, your boy Tyler is right," Mr. Snepp interrupted, settling his black funeral hat firmly over his red hair. "Oat is waiting on me, sure enough, and will start to fret if I'm not home by nightfall."

Mama nodded approvingly, as if she admired the fact Mr. Snepp was so considerate of his young ones. "Well, then, I'll put some meat and potatoes together, and you can eat them as you ride along," she said. "They'll be cold, but with a little salt to season them, they'll taste mighty good."

"You were right about Lucas being good help," Mr. Snepp said, turning to Tyler to make conversation while Mama fixed up the meal. Tyler noticed that he himself was addressed as if he were the man of the house. *Good!* Because if the need arose, it would make it easier to speak frankly to Mr. Snepp about keeping to his own side of Sweet Creek from now on.

"And your friend Isaac, too—both of 'em were fine companions." Tyler was annoyed to see how the words puffed Lucas up; even Isaac seemed pleased. "When the weather turns, I'll bring my team on over and help you put in that hemp crop."

Tyler stiffened. "I reckon Mama and me will have to talk it over," he said coolly.

"Oh, Mr. Snepp told me and Isaac that him and Mama already talked about it when they were burying Mrs. Snepp," Lucas put in. The remark made Mr. Snepp turn scarlet. To cover his embarrassment he hastily handed a newspaper to Tyler.

"I brought you something special, too, son."

I am NOT your son! Tyler wanted to object.

"Your uncle Matt must have put a notice about your papa in the New Hope paper," Mr. Snepp went on, "because the publisher in McMinnville picked it up and ran it, too." Tyler took the paper without a word. He should have been grateful Mr. Snepp had thought of him, just as he'd thought of everyone else. He wasn't. He felt more peeved than ever.

Only after Mr. Snepp's wagon finally clattered across the bridge did Tyler spread the newspaper on the table and search for the article about Papa. He found it on the second page, in a black-bordered box in the right-hand corner, and was pleased to note how carefully it had been prepared, as if Papa were a man of some importance. He read it aloud to the whole family.

"John Bohannon, a resident of Sweet Creek and lately a captain in Gen. Joseph O. Shelby's Iron Brigade of Missouri, has been reported to have passed away in the country of Brazil. (*Dear readers:* Brazil is on the west coast of South America—*Your editor.*) Mr. Bohannon, as many of you will remember, was called 'Black Jack' by all his friends. He will be sorely missed in these parts. He was a fine judge of horseflesh and known to be an expert shot. He leaves behind a widow, Ellen; a daughter, Rosa Lee; and two sons, Tyler and Lucas."

The stove cracked merrily, but the kitchen fell into silence. "Was my name spelled out?" Rosa Lee finally asked, just as she'd asked about the letter Papa's friend William Emerson had written. Again, Tyler showed her, and she traced her name carefully.

"And you and me are right here, Lucas," Tyler said.

Lucas also touched the page. "Seems to make it real, don't it, Ty?" he murmured. The tone of his voice was matter-of-fact. It held no sound of heartbreak, no hint of rusty tears. "I mean, if a person can read it in a newspaper, then it's really real."

How peculiar . . . it was as if he and Lucas had suddenly changed places. Now it was Lucas who was eager to accept that life would always be different. Lucas was even excited about Mr. Snepp's doggone hemp! Over and over, Lucas had said, "It ain't fair"; now, Tyler realized, *he* was the one who longed to utter that same wail.

As Tyler wrestled with his thoughts, Isaac hunched over the table and inspected the newspaper, too. "Show me what you just read, Ty," he asked timidly. Tyler pointed out the black-bordered item. Isaac stared at it. "Must be a fine thing to be able to read," he said, running his finger under the lines of text.

"You could learn, same as me and Lucas," Tyler said gruffly.

"Not likely," Isaac said with a sigh. "Like I tol' you, boys kept up at the Big House to do chores sometimes learned to read. Mostly, though, black folk got in a peck of trouble tryin' to do that. Master didn't hold with us learnin' anything about words or numbers or such. Said it made us uppity and gave us bad ideas."

Tyler set his jaw. A fierce determination suddenly blazed like a stirred-up bonfire inside him. He'd just had to put up with Elway and his hemp . . . he'd had to accept that look on Mama's face when she smiled at Mr. Snepp . . . but the war was over now and he didn't have to put up with folks tromping on Isaac's rights.

"Well, that's goin' to change—starting tomorrow," he declared.

"Can't see how," Isaac said, refolding the newspaper. "Ol' Isaac ain't goin' to learn to read in his sleep tonight!"

"You're goin' to school with Lucas and me in the morning," Tyler announced. "Mr. Blackburn teaches us how to read—well, he might as well teach you, too."

"That might not be such a good idea, Ty," Isaac protested softly.

Tyler brushed the warning aside. "Don't see why not."

Isaac gave him a long glance, then peered at the newspaper in his hand. Slowly, a smile bloomed on his wide, dark face. "Imagine—Isaac Peerce learnin' to read! Now wouldn't my kin be surprised!"

Chapter Thirteen

WHEN THE BOYS SET OUT FOR SCHOOL after the long holiday vacation, Sooner invited himself along. Before, he'd seemed to understand his place was at home with Mama and Rosa Lee, but seeing Isaac trek off must have made him decide he'd be welcome, too.

"No! Go back, Sooner!" Tyler commanded, and pointed sternly in the direction of the cabin. Sooner studied him with a thoughtful blue eye and a merry brown one, then flopped on his belly in the middle of the road.

"Home, Sooner! *Go home!*" Tyler yelled. Sooner wagged his tail cheerfully, sculpting half-circles in the dusty road, but declined to obey.

"Aw, it can't hurt anything if he comes with us," Lucas begged. As if he understood that Lucas was taking his side, Sooner hopped to his feet as though permission were about to be granted.

"Lucas, you know as well as me there's always a pack of dogs hanging around down there at school," Tyler argued. "Mean sons o' guns that like to fight. I don't want Sooner getting into a tussle and coming out on the wrong end of it like happened to Mr. Blackburn's hound Rafe last year."

Tyler stalked up the road, grabbed Sooner by the ruff of the neck, and hauled him back to the porch. "Mama, you see that he stays home," he shouted through the door.

"Better bring him inside then," Mama called back, "so's I can keep an eye on him." Tyler opened the door just far enough to shove Sooner through, then slammed it shut quick. On the other side, he heard Sooner set up a howl of dismay.

"It's for your own good," Tyler yelled over his shoulder, but Sooner was carrying on so loud he couldn't have heard thunder, much less an explanation.

Lately, before Mr. Blackburn rang the bell each morning to call everyone into Two Mile school, Oat Snepp had taken to lounging against the fence with Joshua Simons, the biggest kid at school. The moment Oat saw Tyler, Lucas, and Isaac, he called out in that superior tone of voice that Tyler detested. "Your mama had only three dollars for a mule!" he taunted. "So how come all of a sudden she's so well-off she sends you to school with your own personal servant?"

At the sneer in Oat's voice, Isaac immediately took a step back, half turned, poised on the balls of his feet, ready to hit for home. Tyler grabbed him by the sleeve and pulled him along. Mama sure made a mistake feeling sorry for Oat! It was plain that burying his own mother hadn't humbled him a whit.

"You know full well we don't keep servants," Tyler retorted. "Isaac—well, Isaac's working for us." Of course it wasn't true; no payment for services had ever been discussed with Isaac and no money had ever changed hands.

"So if he's workin' for you, Bohannon, then what's he doin' down here at Two Mile school?"

This time it wasn't Oat but Joshua Simons who demanded to know more. He lived at the lower end of

Sweet Creek, near where it emptied into the Welcome River. Not only was he the tallest kid in school, Tyler often thought he was the dullest witted as well. He also weighed as much as most grown men.

"Isaac is goin' to learn some letters and numbers, not that it's any of your beeswax," Lucas spoke up, pleased to throw in his two cents' worth.

"We'll just see what Mr. Blackburn says about that!" Oat exclaimed.

"Then we'll find out right now, won't we?" Tyler threw back, and hustled Isaac through the door into the single large classroom of Two Mile school. Mr. Blackburn glanced up with mild surprise when Tyler led Isaac toward his desk.

"Mr. Blackburn, this here is Isaac, who is staying with us Bohannons for a while," Tyler announced. "You know about the Freedman's Act, don't you?" Mr. Blackburn blinked and nodded his head dazedly. "Well, I figure it means Isaac can go to school for a spell. He'll have to sit with the kids in the lower grades, but he's willing to do that. Ain't you, Isaac?" Isaac mumbled "Yes," but kept his eyes fastened on the floor. "Main thing is, Isaac wants to learn to read and write and maybe do sums."

Mr. Blackburn, by nature a colorless sort of man, turned a paler shade of pale. "Well now, Tyler, I don't know—"

"Oh, it's all right," Tyler assured him. "My mama will see to it that Isaac's got clean clothes and will make him a lunch and all. He won't be an extra burden to you. All you got to do is teach him, same's you teach me and Lucas and the rest of us."

Mr. Blackburn cleared his throat. "What I mean is—well, Tyler, black folks and white folks in the same school together? Is that what the Freedman's Act said?" Tyler had never stopped to wonder what it actually said. Shoot! Free meant free, didn't it?

"The problem is, Tyler, there'll be some of your classmates—not to mention their mamas and daddies—who won't like it one bit that your . . . ah, um . . . friend is going to sit down right next to white folk."

Tyler realized he'd have to stand his ground as he had to stand it when Mama wanted to make Isaac sleep in the cow shed. Just the same, he was puzzled. During the war, Mr. Blackburn hadn't sided with either North or South. He even kept a picture of Abe Lincoln pinned up on the wall right along with Jefferson Davis. Why was he so skittish now?

"We just fought a whole long war over this," Tyler reminded him. "My daddy fought in it, and Oat Snepp's brother Billy died in it. They were on the losing side—and now black folks are supposed to be free. Well, that must mean they're free to go to school, too."

Mr. Blackburn clutched his large pale hands together as if in prayer. "What you say is true, Tyler. Yet I fear there's going to be a mighty lot of trouble over what you're asking me to do."

"Won't know till we try, will we?" Tyler insisted, amazed at the steel in his own backbone. Finally, Mr. Blackburn bowed his head and slowly turned the pages of his attendance book. "Well. I suppose I could enter your friend's name here in pencil, just in case he isn't able to stay in class very long. Ah . . . um . . . does Isaac have a last name, like regular folks?"

"He surely does," Tyler said. "It's Peerce, with two *e*'s."

A moment later, when Mr. Blackburn rang the bell to call everyone indoors, Mary Chesney and her sister Luella hugged the wall the minute they set eyes on Isaac. Tyler was disgusted. A person would swear they'd never seen a black person in their whole lives, which, considering this was Missouri, he doubted could be true. Little Danny Ellis, who was in the first grade and might never have seen a black person up close, touched Isaac's hand and asked if the paint ever rubbed off.

"Nossir," Isaac said, smiling faintly. "It don't rub off, wouldn't even if I was to wash and wash with the strongest lye soap your mama's got."

"Whoa!" Joshua Simons said when he spied Isaac sitting in the corner beside Danny and Essie Murphy, the only first graders at Two Mile school. Isaac looked a trifle foolish at a desk much too small for him, his knees tucked up under his chin, his elbows crooked out like chicken wings. "I don't aim to go to school with no black boy," Joshua spluttered, glaring first at Isaac, then at Tyler, lastly at Mr. Blackburn. "Don't have to. Won't do it, neither."

"Children, children," Mr. Blackburn soothed, and managed to shush everyone. He even coaxed Mary and Luella into their seats, and the morning went along uneventfully. Out of the corner of his eye, Tyler watched as Isaac paid careful attention when Mr. Blackburn showed Essie how to print her name on the slate at the front of the room. Isaac would have a lot of catching up to do, he thought with a smile, but when they got back home he'd give him extra help.

At noon, after everyone had gobbled down their lunches (Mama put cold potatoes, squares of corn bread, and pieces of dried apple in the lunch she'd packed for Tyler and Lucas to share with Isaac), all the students tumbled outside. The thaw that began after New Year's Day had melted the snow and now filled the air with a springlike smell, making everyone at Two Mile school feel a little giddy.

Oat Snepp and Joshua Simons returned to sentry

duty along the fence, arms hooked back over it, and watched with squinty eyes when Tyler and Isaac came out to sit on the steps. Lucas ran off to torment Mary and Luella, who made sure he caught them once in a while so they'd have a chance to shriek with gleeful terror.

"Them two boys over there be lookin' at us mighty evil," Isaac whispered. He studied his feet to avoid looking directly at Oat and Joshua. "I know what them kinda looks mean, Ty. I seen 'em whenever black folks step outta line."

"You haven't stepped out of line or done anything for them to give you the evil eye," Tyler scoffed. "They must've eaten something at lunch that didn't agree with 'em." His own heart flopped anxiously against his ribs, though. To be honest, he hadn't figured bringing Isaac to school would cause such a ruckus. Isaac was free, wasn't he? Then why couldn't he—

Tyler's heart did another flop when Oat and Joshua sauntered in his and Isaac's direction, hands hooked in their belts, heads tipped back like a pair of sheriffs on official business. "C'mon, Isaac," Tyler whispered. "We'll go back inside. No sense giving them a chance to start trouble."

"You some kind of scaredy cat, Bohannon?" Joshua called as he and Isaac rose off the step.

"Takes one to know one," Tyler shot back.

"I aim to tell my pa what you brought to school today," Joshua threatened.

"I didn't bring a *what*," Tyler snapped. He was pleased that he couldn't hear a hint of fear in his voice even though his heart was doing somersaults under his breastbone.

"What's that s'posed to mean?" Joshua demanded.

"I brought a *who*, that's what it means. A person. Get it? A *what* is a thing. Isaac ain't a thing. Haven't you been listening when Mr. Blackburn has us do grammar?"

"My pa ain't goin' to like it, Bohannon," Joshua insisted. "He won't be pleased with Mr. Blackburn for lettin' your darky into school, neither. My pa wasn't for the Union any more'n yours was."

Privately, Tyler admitted it was a little hard to reconcile that fact in his own head. After all, Papa had sided with those who wanted to keep black folks in chains. Somehow, though, he knew Papa would be on his side in this matter. Papa hadn't liked those folks in the North laying down the law to him—but he wouldn't like Mr. Simons or Joshua doing it, either.

When they got home in the afternoon, Mama wanted to know how Isaac's first day of school had gone, and Tyler lied with keen conviction. "Oh, it was fine, Mama." Isaac was silent, however. Tyler went on, "Isaac has to sit with the little kids, though, where he looks sort of silly, with his knees folded up under his chin."

Isaac smiled uncertainly. "Yes'm, I looked a little silly all right. So maybe I won't go back tomorrow."

"Of course you will," Tyler declared. No way were Oat Snepp and Joshua Simons going to wreck Isaac's chance to learn to read and write. Suddenly, Tyler figured he knew exactly how Papa felt about the war: that nobody had the right to tell him what he could or couldn't do.

The next morning, after Sooner had the door shut in his face for the second day in a row, Tyler, Lucas, and Isaac walked the mile to school. There, Oat and Joshua hung against the fence as usual, their eyes even narrower than yesterday. At lunchtime, Tyler wasn't surprised when the trouble started all over again.

"My pa says if that darky shows up one more time,

he'll ride straight up here and put things a-right," Joshua promised. "He says it ain't fit black and white should be in school together. Best you send 'im home, Bohannon, before my pa gets *really* mad." Joshua poked the toe of his boot in Isaac's direction. "If you was smart, darky, you'd be on your way before we go inside for afternoon class."

Isaac looked at Tyler. "I know my way back, Ty. It be best if I—"

"You ain't goin' nowhere!" Tyler said through gritted teeth. Joshua edged a little closer and poked his boot in Isaac's direction again. "You, Simons, quit ragging on him, hear me?" Tyler ordered.

"Or else what?" Joshua Simons taunted. "What'll you do if I don't?" He swung his foot in an arc, an inch from Isaac's shin bone.

"Leave him be," Oat Snepp croaked, as if he suddenly realized things were about to take a turn he hadn't counted on. "Shoot, it don't matter if—"

"It *does* matter," Joshua hissed. "You said so yourself, not five minutes ago! Said you didn't want to go to school with no black boy any more'n I did."

Oat shot a glance in Tyler's direction, and Tyler knew what had happened. For some reason, uppity Oat Snepp wanted to make an impression on Joshua and had woven a web for himself that now held him fast. He couldn't unsay whatever he'd said to Joshua earlier, and now Joshua intended to hold him to his word.

Joshua reached out with a grimy paw that hadn't made friends with a washbowl in a long while and gave Isaac a shove. It was plain Isaac had been shoved before because he caught his balance nimbly. Joshua pushed him harder the second time, causing Isaac to do a funny little soft-shoe dance to right himself.

"You deaf, or what?" Tyler yelled. "I said, quit ragging

on 'im!" The loudness of his voice caused Lucas to stop chasing Mary and Luella and come running to find out what was going on.

Joshua Simons whirled, and—being four inches taller—had to bend down to stick his face into Tyler's. "Well, if it ain't Abe Lincoln hisself! You remember what happened to *him,* don't you? Somebody shot him in the head and killed him dead, in case you forgot. So shut your mouth, Bohannon, or I'll shut it for you."

Tyler drew himself up as tall as he could, but the four-inch difference between him and Joshua didn't change more than a hair. "Go ahead," he said, surprised to hear himself issue such a bold invitation. "Because I'm not goin' to shut my mouth. I aim to see Isaac goes into class soon as Mr. Blackburn rings the bell."

Joshua Simons didn't need a second invitation. With his grubby hand knotted into a loose fist, he smacked Tyler across the jaw. "Lay off my brother!" Lucas screeched, and flew into action, his own fists whirling like windmill blades. Joshua shoved Lucas out of the way as if he were no more irksome than a gnat.

"Whoa, Joshua," Oat soothed. "Like I said, I don't think—"

"You don't think what?" Joshua demanded loudly. "You turned into a chicken-hearted girl, or what?"

"Girls don't have chicken hearts!" Mary and Luella Chesney shrieked from the sidelines. By now everyone at Two Mile school had gathered around, Danny and Essie included. Mr. Blackburn hurried out to stand on the school step, wringing his pale hands as if he couldn't make up his mind what to do or say.

Tyler shot a glance in Oat's direction and saw his face was contorted with doubt. Maybe he was remembering how Mama had gone over to wash his own mother's body for burial so she'd be presentable for a decent laying-out in the Snepp parlor. Maybe he was recalling how Mama stayed an extra night to wipe away the tears of his little brothers, put them to bed like his own mother used to, had told them the story about Jack and the Beanstalk until they fell into an easy sleep.

"You had enough?" Joshua demanded. "You goin' to send your darky boy back home to do chores, which is the only thing a darky's good for? Any fool knows schoolin' don't do black folks no good. Puts ideas in their heads—and my pa says there ain't anything worse'n an uppity darky."

"Isaac ain't goin' home," Tyler mumbled. He touched his jaw where it was turning numb and felt a swelling rise under his fingertips. Before he'd even dropped his hand, Joshua popped him again, this time on the other side. "Had enough now?" he yelled.

"Quit!" Oat cried desperately. "No need to make a mess outta him, Simons. Just let it go!"

Joshua brushed Oat's words aside. "Ain't about to let it go," he vowed, and raised his fist a third time. He didn't get a chance to use it because from out of nowhere a blazing red demon hurtled through the air, struck Joshua smack in the chest, and knocked him flat.

Sooner!

The dog straddled his quarry, his front paws on either side of Joshua's neck, his lips pulled back to show rows of gleaming teeth, his nose touching Joshua's. The terrible growl that came up from deep in his belly even chilled Tyler's blood. Sooner's blue eye fixed Joshua with the cool, impersonal stare of a judge meting out a verdict. The brown one warned him that in another second he might get a chunk taken off the end of his beak.

Joshua covered his face with his hands. "It's a devil!"

he shrieked. "Git 'im offa me! Git that devil off before I'm killed!"

Tyler seized Sooner by the neck and pulled him aside. "Ain't no devil, Simons. It's only a dog," he said. Somehow, Sooner must have gotten away from Mama, then had followed them straight to school. He'd seen Joshua raise his fist, had slunk across the school yard without anyone seeing him—not even the strays that lurked around the yard hoping to snatch up lunch scraps from the likes of Essie and Danny—then had launched himself through the air like something out of a nightmare. Tyler smiled to himself. Sooner aimed to make up for not being able to handle the scalawags!

Joshua Simons peered out from under his dirty hands. "Don't look like any reg'lar dawg to me!" he howled. "Them eyes—them are devil eyes!"

"Naw," Tyler scoffed. "He's just a mutt that belongs to Lucas and me. Lots of dogs in Scotland have eyes just like 'em." Lucas grinned proudly to be identified as Sooner's part owner.

Joshua scrambled to his feet.

"I'm goin' to tell my pa you're keeping a mad dawg up there at your place! I'll tell 'im it came at me and was foamin' at the mouth!" he screeched. "He'll bring his rifle when he comes to straighten Mr. Blackburn out, and he'll take care of that devil dawg while he's at it!"

"Not unless he kills me first," Tyler vowed, remembering how easily Bigger had been slain.

"Hafta shoot me, too!" Lucas chimed in eagerly.

"Me, too!" Oat shouted unexpectedly.

"I'm goin' to take Sooner home now, Simons," Tyler said. "You go back into school. I'll make sure he doesn't come back again—on account of next time you might not be so lucky."

Joshua backed toward the step, where Mr. Blackburn moaned helplessly and flapped his large white hands as if they were dishcloths he hoped to shake dry. As Tyler dragged Sooner from the school yard, Oat leaned close.

"I didn't know Joshua was going to take on like he did," he confessed. "But I reckon you better think about all the trouble you're causin', Bohannon. You want Isaac to read and write so bad?—well, then maybe you oughta teach him yourself."

Tyler shot Oat a disgusted look. "What's right is right," he retorted. "Isaac ain't nobody's slave. If he wants some schooling, ain't no good reason why he can't have it—whether Joshua Simons likes it or not!"

Lucas stayed at school, but Isaac hustled along beside Tyler as they headed for Sweet Creek. When they were well out of earshot of those who watched their departure, he reminded Tyler of Oat's suggestion. "On account of no matter what you say, Ty, I ain't never goin' back with you tomorrow or any other day," he said.

There was a note in his voice that surprised Tyler. Isaac clearly had made up his own mind about the matter, and Tyler realized it would be useless to argue with him. Somehow, Isaac's no-nonsense air made him seem older, wiser, and soon Tyler found it was he who was hustling to keep up as they strode for home.

"If you teach me yourself, it won't cause any pain or strain to a single soul," Isaac declared. "Not Mr. Blackburn, not you or me, not nobody. Not even ol' Sooner!" Hearing his name, Sooner wagged his tail proudly, as if he knew he'd redeemed himself after his miserable encounter with the scalawags.

Tyler clamped his jaw. "But it ain't right, Isaac, you bein' thrown out of school like that on the say-so of a no-account like Joshua Simons."

Isaac shrugged. "Maybe it be too early, Ty—and Joshua ain't as no-account as you think! He's like most folks who ain't over the war yet. Anyway, don't take on the same way your pa did. He set his heart on an impossible idea, too. Hugged it to his breast like it was his best friend—you tol' me so yourself."

Tyler stared at Isaac. What right did he have to talk about Papa that way? Who'd he think he was? For a split second Tyler had half a mind to take a poke at Isaac himself!

"Why, you uppity—" he blurted, then stopped short, astonished at what he'd almost said.

Uppity darky . . . that's what was on the tip of his tongue. Was it possible that in the blink of an eye he'd changed places with no-account Joshua Simons? Isaac faced him, and to Tyler's horror, the swift, knowing look that darkened the black boy's eyes told him it was true.

Thought you was different, din't you, Ty Bohannon? But you ain't. You be safe in your white skin, not even realizin' how powerful easy it be to say such hurtful words! Isaac's glance accused silently.

"Listen, Isaac, that ain't what I really meant," Tyler said hastily. "I didn't aim for it to come out soundin' like that. It's one of those things people say without thinking first. They don't really—" But Isaac turned away at the gate and headed on down to the cow shed.

"I'll milk tonight," he called brusquely over his shoulder.

Tyler watched Isaac go with a heart that felt like a stone. Oh, if only he could stuff those words back in his mouth! He'd swallow them whole, wouldn't even stop to chew. Slowly, it dawned on Tyler what he'd done. The same thing Oat had: He'd said something that now couldn't be unsaid, had woven a web that now held him fast.

Chapter Fourteen

YOU UPPITY DARKY . . .

Tyler cringed. How could those three words have leaped into his head as handily as frogs onto a lily pad? He felt his bowels churn as he recalled the stricken look in Isaac's eyes. *You be safe in your white skin, boy,* that look said. *Which makes me exactly like Joshua Simons,* Tyler realized. Uppity darky; those words—so easy to say, so hurtful to hear—had been part of him just as they were part of a tub of lard like Joshua.

Sorry was too feeble a word to sum up Tyler's remorse. The only thing to do now was just try to go ahead. It was Isaac himself who'd come up with the only possible solution to what had happened today: He couldn't—wouldn't, no matter how much he wanted to learn to read—ever go back to Two Mile school again. So after Mama and Rosa Lee cleared the supper table, Tyler got out some paper, a pencil, and beckoned Isaac to sit down.

"You're right, Isaac. Oat was, too." He hoped Isaac would look him right in the eye so that he could apologize with a glance. Isaac kept his head bowed and refused to give him the chance.

"I *can* teach you to read and write," Tyler vowed. Eventually, maybe Isaac would be willing to let bygones be bygones. "We'll leave sums till later, though, on account of I've never been a teacher before."

"Isaac never been to school before, so we're startin' out even," Isaac murmured. When he finally lifted his glance, Tyler saw behind his dark eyes thoughts that couldn't be read. Was Isaac remembering curses from the master who'd left that scar on his cheek? *Truth is, I'm stuck inside my white skin and he's stuck inside his black one,* Tyler realized. *We can't trade places; no way can we know what it's like to be the other one.*

Tyler painstakingly began to print the alphabet at the top of the page. He sounded out each letter for Isaac as he wrote.

"All the words we say—just like the ones I'm using to you right this very minute, Isaac—are made up of these twenty-six letters," Tyler explained. "Putting the letters together in different ways makes different words."

Sooner, lying near the wood box, was lulled by the soft murmur and started to snore contentedly. Rosa Lee's interest was piqued, though, and she came to hang on the corner of the table to watch what was going on.

"For instance, if a person takes these three letters," Tyler continued, pointing to *d, o,* and *g,* "he can make a word that spells *dog.*" He printed *dog* on the page. To Isaac, it seemed like magic.

"You can just take that . . . and that . . . and that— and out comes a dog!" he exclaimed. Isaac seemed to have put the episode on the road out of his mind for a moment and was as tickled as if the letters had sprouted ears, legs, and a tail that wagged. Tyler picked out other three-letter words—*cat* and *hat, boy* and *toy, gun* and *sun*—and printed them out as well.

"I want writing lessons, too!" Rosa Lee declared, no longer satisfied to listen while Isaac was instructed. As was her nature, she gave Tyler a ferocious scowl when he didn't immediately comply with her request.

"Tyler's got his hands full teaching one student at a time," Mama soothed. "Anyway, you'll be starting school next year." Rosa Lee sighed, rested her elbows on the table, and settled for being an observer.

"Know something, Ty? They's two words I'd like to learn how to spell straight off," Isaac murmured after Tyler made longer words—*cabin* and *creek*, *horse* and *wagon, rabbit* and *raccoon*.

"Which ones?" Tyler asked.

"Isaac Peerce," Isaac replied softly. "More'n anything, I'd like to write my own name. That way, nobody'd ever have to make a mark for me again, like they did for all my kin."

"Shoot, that won't be hard," Tyler answered, and carefully printed

ISAAC PEERCE

in large block letters in the middle of the paper. "There it is," he said. "That's what you look like. *You*, Isaac Peerce, plain as day."

Isaac touched his fingertip to each letter. "Me," he murmured, his voice filled with awe. "There I am. Isaac Peerce. Won't have to be an *X* no more."

Tyler identified each of the letters in Isaac's name in the alphabet at the top of the page, then gave Isaac the pencil. "For practice, you copy each one just like I wrote 'em here." He showed Isaac how to draw a vertical line with a bar at the top and another bar at the bottom. "That's an *I,* Isaac, and it's the first letter of your name."

Next he showed Isaac how to make a swoopy, curved *S,* then two *A*'s like teepees with a brace in the middle to hold them steady, and finally a *C* like the crescent moon. "You practice on 'em awhile, then we'll work on *Peerce,*" Tyler said.

Isaac hunched over the table, his head so low his nose nearly touched the paper. He carefully began to copy each letter. While he labored over his assignment, Tyler finished his geography lesson, then picked up the newspaper Mr. Snepp had left behind with the announcement about Papa. Mama had already cut out the black-bordered item on page two and said she'd keep it safe in the Bible next to her bed.

On the front page was a headline announcing that some men back in Washington wanted to impeach President Andy Johnson because they didn't like how he was reconstructing the South after the war. A small article at the corner of the page described a new club with a peculiar name that some folks down in Tennessee had gotten up. Ku Klux Klan, they called it. It looked sort of funny with three *K*'s right in a row like that. On the back page was an article about a place called the Territory of Dakota.

"The West stretches farther west every day," Tyler read silently. "Americans of all ages are looking toward the territories for new opportunities. Rumor has it that there are jobs aplenty, that land is cheap, and hundreds are traveling there every month."

Tyler folded the paper and laid it aside with his geography lesson. He wondered what a territory looked like. It sounded bigger than a plain old state. As if there was more air and sky out there. Was there, really? That business about people of all ages heading out that way; well, maybe it would be all right for Joshua Simons, who was already more man than boy, but why would an ordinary boy ever want to leave home? Tyler thought about the top of the hill, where Papa's spirit had been put to rest. He aimed to be laid up there himself someday. No way did he intend to ever leave Missouri for a place called a territory.

Tyler was glad it turned out to be a year when spring came early. On a bright, warm Saturday morning that made him think about hitching Patches up and doing a little plowing, a rattle of wagon wheels on the bridge caused everyone at the breakfast table to pause, spoons of mush halfway to their mouths. Sooner set up a cheerful ruckus and scratched at the door, his tail wagging wildly. Tyler hoped it wasn't who he thought it was, but when Mama murmured softly, "Why, I think it's Elway!" everyone spilled out of the cabin to welcome him.

Tyler stayed put at the table and gritted his teeth.

The man's name is Mr. Snepp, he wanted to remind the whole lot of them. *Fools! Don't go calling him Elway like that.* It sounded way too friendly to be proper. Anyway, what sort of name was it? *El-way*—a fussy, fidgety name, nothing like Black Jack, which had lots of flash and dash to it.

Before Mama hurried outside, Tyler noticed how swiftly she smoothed her hair back, how she frowned as she pressed the wrinkles out of her apron by flattening it against herself with her palms. Mr. Snepp might have a fussy name, but for some reason she intended to make a good impression on him.

Tyler's teeth ached when he suspected what might be in her heart, then he felt reassured by her frown. Mr. Snepp had just been widowed; Mama was only trying to be a good neighbor and obviously was a bit annoyed to have her morning's work interrupted with unexpected company.

There was the sound of many other voices outside besides Mr. Snepp's, and finally curiosity got the better of Tyler. He broke a splinter off a piece of firewood. Using it as a toothpick, he sauntered outside and slouched against the door frame. He cleaned his teeth methodically, studying the visitors with a cool eye. It provoked him to see Sooner was still wagging his red tail merrily as if everyone were actually welcome.

Mr. Snepp certainly hadn't arrived alone. The whole wagon was full of children. His own; all boys, of course. Tyler didn't know their names but discovered to his thorough disgust that Mama did.

"My, Seth, you look fine today," she said, her voice an octave higher and more cheerful than it had in a long while. "And so does Saul," she said to the little chap's red-haired twin. She rattled off the names of all the others as well. A very small boy in a too-large hand-me-down red shirt was named Henry. There was a good-sized chap, though not as old as Oat, who was called Elijah; she addressed a lad halfway in between all the others as James; another boy toward the bottom of the ladder was named Benjamin.

Seven Snepps in all, if a person counted Oat, who sat beside his father on the wagon bench and didn't look any happier than Tyler felt. The four youngest boys piled out of the wagon and flocked around Mama, pulling on her apron or tugging at her sleeve, each one starved for a word from her or a pat on the head. Tyler saw her frown change to a smile as she studied each one with tender concern.

"If your boys are willing to pitch in, Miz Bohannon, I thought this would be a fine day to put in that hemp crop for you," Mr. Snepp said. He lifted his hat and his chipmunk cheeks pouched out when he grinned. She might call him Elway, but *he* had the good sense to address her as Mrs. Bohannon. Tyler's ire subsided. The man knew his place after all.

Just the same, Tyler heard himself declare firmly, "I don't believe we've decided to plant any, Mr. Snepp." He flicked his toothpick away and rested his fists on his hips.

"Well, son, I believe we ought to try at least a small patch of it," Mama spoke up just as firmly, overruling him without calling him aside to discuss the matter privately. "Then, if it turns out to be as good a crop as Elway says, why, we can plant more next year." Tyler felt his cheeks blaze. He couldn't believe what she'd just done! He was trying to be the man of the house, but she treated his opinion as if it made no more difference than Lucas's.

Tyler watched bitterly as Mr. Snepp took his plowshare out of the back of the wagon and set about unhitching his team from the wagon so he could get them ready to work. Patches, who'd been walking faithfully up and down the road in front of the cabin twice a day ever since the weather began to get warm, brayed plaintively as if to complain he'd been training hard so he could do the job himself.

Mr. Snepp's mules looked glossier than when Tyler had seen them the first time. Had Elway Snepp taken special pains to brush and groom them in order to make an impression on Mama?

Lucas and Isaac—a pair of witless nincompoops!—pitched right in to help Oat and Mr. Snepp with the harnesses, then trailed up the hillside along with everyone else. Rosa Lee treated the whole affair as if it were a party arranged especially for her. She lined the smaller boys up on the porch and poured pretend tea for them out of a cracked pot Mama had given her. Mama herself hurried indoors, and Tyler realized she intended to get started on a noonday meal for all those motherless boys.

Lordy, lordy. It was just too much.

"Aren't you going on up to help with the planting?" Mama called when Tyler didn't budge from his place on the porch.

"No, I surely ain't!" he declared. "Don't think anybody'll miss me, either!"

Tyler jumped off down the steps and strode off to the cow shed. He grabbed a bridle, settled it roughly over Patches's tall ears, and climbed on his bony back.

"Doggone three-dollar mule!" he said through gritted teeth as he urged Patches briskly along the edge of the creek. "Goin' over to the Snepps' to get you was the saddest trip I ever made in my life! Lookit all the trouble you caused!"

Of course the words were no sooner out of his mouth than he felt like a fool. None of it was Patches's fault, and he apologized by patting the old boy's neck. "Oh, none of it's your doing," he groaned, "any more'n it's any of mine—but all them Snepps hanging around just ain't right, Patches. All right, so they got no mama—well, let 'em go shop for one somewhere else!"

Tyler crossed the mule to the other side of the creek at a place where the water was no more than a trickle, then went straight up to where Papa's spirit was. He slid off Patches's back and let him graze on the fresh shoots of new spring grass.

He studiously averted his gaze from the sight of everyone else working on the slope below. Just the same, their merry calls back and forth, punctuated by Sooner's gleeful yipping, made Tyler feel lonelier than ever. Worse even than the morning he'd waited on the opposite side of the Rio Grande while Papa rode off to Mexico. This time, though, there wasn't even a loyal dog like Bigger to hang on to. That red fool, Sooner—just as big an idiot as Lucas and Isaac!—was only too happy to be down there in the midst of all the excitement.

Tyler laid back and studied the sky. It was streaked with mare's tail clouds, and behind him, he could hear chickadees calling sweetly from the pines. He sifted through the events of the past few months. Fetching Patches home . . . Isaac arriving with the letter from William Emerson . . . laying Papa to rest . . . scalawags figuring to rob the family of everything it owned . . . Oat's mother dying . . . Mr. Snepp making a gift of hemp seed to Mama . . . trying to take Isaac to school . . . old tub-of-lard Joshua Simons ruining everything . . .

Such a jumble. It was hard to make heads or tails of anything anymore. Just when a person got ready to accept how life could go on even without Papa, the world changed again in ways you never counted on. Cheerful voices continued to waft up the hillside, but again Tyler closed his ears and his heart to their sound. Let Elway Snepp plow furrows to the moon for all he cared.

After the Snepps finally went home and the cabin descended into blessed quiet again, Mama said there was something she wanted to tell everyone. Isaac excused himself, but Mama urged him to stay. "This concerns you, too, Isaac," she said. "After all, you're more or less part of the family now." She smiled at him, and Tyler saw it wasn't a fake smile, either.

He was pleased to note there were blue smudges of weariness beneath Mama's eyes. Fine! It meant the rowdy, noisy herd of Snepps had worn her out. On the other hand, her face was soft, and there was a disturbing ease in her glance.

"Children, Elway Snepp has asked me to marry him," she announced. She said it straight out, didn't even preface the words with other ones that would make the bitter pill easier to swallow. "He says his children need a mother, and he thinks he can be a good father to mine."

"No!" Tyler exploded. "It ain't fitting! Mr. Snepp's been widowed hardly any time at all. Besides, we only found out about Papa at Christmastime. It's way too soon! So maybe his children need a mother—but *we* sure don't need a father!" The harshness of his words made Sooner rise from his station at the wood box. The hackles raised menacingly on his neck; he growled and walked stiff-legged toward the door as if he suspected scalawags were lurking on the other side.

"You quit bein' so mean, Ty!" Rosa Lee objected. "I like playing with Seth and Saul—even if I can't always tell which is which!"

"And Mr. Snepp did us a mighty good turn helping us put in that hemp crop today," Lucas reminded Tyler.

Why was Lucas, of all people, being so reasonable? Tyler fumed and became even more peeved when Lucas suddenly asked Mama where they'd all live after the wedding. As if a wedding were already a done deal!

"Elway has a big house," Mama said, "with room enough for all of us. He says we should put our two parcels of land together, just like we'll put our two families together. Elway says someday you boys will be able to farm this place for yourselves."

Tyler stared down at his hands. He'd clenched them so hard the knuckles had turned white. It was plain Mama and Mr. Snepp had discussed a lot more than hemp.

They'd figured it all out between them: who would live where, how the land should be taken care of, what would happen someday to the place at Sweet Creek.

Mama hadn't set them down to tell them there *might* be a wedding. She'd already decided there would be.

"So when do you aim to do it?" Tyler asked tonelessly.

"Elway says it takes a hundred days for a hemp crop to mature. He says right after it's harvested would be a good time," Mama said. *Elway says, Elway says!* All of a sudden, everything was *Elway says,* as if the family didn't know how to make its own way till he showed up.

"That will give me plenty of time to make new dresses for Rosa Lee and me, and to let your uncle Matt know about the wedding," she finished with a tired, satisfied smile. "There'll be time to make arrangements for a minister, so it's all done right and proper."

Right and proper. Except there was nothing right and proper about it. Tyler rose abruptly from the table. Sooner leaped to his feet, too. "It's time for me to milk," Tyler said, though it actually was a little early and would surprise Calico. When Isaac half rose out of his chair, Tyler waved him down and was glad that Lucas didn't offer to help.

"C'mon, Sooner," he commanded gruffly. Sooner ran down the path ahead of him, but Tyler realized he was as faithless as the rest of them. Only reason he was eager to go milk was because he hoped to get a stream of it squirted straight into his mouth.

Tyler hunkered down on the stool and rested his forehead against Calico's comforting haunch. He listened to the rhythmic ping-ping of milk against the sides of the bucket. For some reason, the words from Isaac's hymn drifted through his mind.

You may bury me in the East, You may bury me in the West . . .

The West. But "the West" meant so many different places. It was hard to know exactly where it was. There was California, for instance, facing the western ocean, about as far west as a person could get. There was the Oregon coast, where Mr. Blackburn said Lewis and Clark ate rotten elk meat to celebrate Christmas Day way back in 1805. There were places out there with peculiar names: the Black Hills, Yellowstone River, Beartooth Mountains. Tyler imagined low hills as black as coal . . . a river that washed over bright yellow rocks . . . a range of mountains etched sharply against the sky like a row of bear's teeth.

Never in his life had Tyler dreamed of leaving Sweet Creek. But one hundred days from now, Papa's farm would become someone else's. Mama's last name wouldn't be Bohannon anymore. And lordy, lordy— uppity Oat Snepp would be his brother!

Milk began to fill the pail. What had the McMinnville paper said? Americans of all ages were looking toward the territories for fresh opportunities; there were jobs aplenty and land was cheap. Tyler felt Sooner press urgently against his thigh to remind him about a squirt of warm milk.

"If I go west, you be willin' to come with me?" Tyler demanded sternly. When milk wasn't forthcoming, Sooner whined piteously. "All right; if I give you some, then will you promise—crisscross your heart and hope to die?"

Sooner answered with an assenting bark, his pale eye glowing like a rare, precious stone in the gloom of the shed. Tyler delivered a thin stream of warm milk at him, some of which got into Sooner's mouth, the rest frosting his muzzle with foam.

"Well, I made it down to Texas and back," Tyler muttered. Sooner wasn't listening; he was too busy licking delicious warm foam off his whiskers. "Ain't no reason why I can't make it out to the territories. No reason at all."

Chapter Fifteen

THE HEMP GREW ON SLENDER, rigid stalks about the thickness of a man's finger, and by harvesttime it was more than seven feet tall. Mr. Snepp (no way did Tyler intend to call him Elway until he absolutely had to) had seeded the crop so the plants grew closely together.

"If they're crowded like that," Elway explained, "the stalks will grow tall and the shaft will be bare, with only a crown of foliage at the top." As he spoke, Sooner edged his way into the field to investigate and quickly vanished from sight in the shadowy growth.

"The taller and more leafless the stalk, the better," Mr. Snepp said. "Means we'll get a crop that yields strong, continuous fibers—that's exactly what hemp buyers will pay good money for." Tyler scowled at his use of *we*.

Mr. Snepp pulled up a single stalk, which Tyler saw was ribbed vertically. It was covered with stiff, prickly hairs, almost like a piglet's coat. Elway cut through the stalk with his pocketknife, and Tyler was surprised to see that the woody shaft was hollow. When a strip was peeled lengthwise, however, it came off in a single, silky strand that was fully six feet long.

"This thread can be woven into the finest, strongest rope a man could ask for," Mr. Snepp said, obviously pleased, "or it'll make a piece of the whitest canvas you boys ever saw." He surveyed the field with a satisfied glance, then squinted skyward. "Looks like we can expect several days of dry weather—might as well start to harvest this morning."

"How we goin' to do it?" Lucas wanted to know. Tyler's heart felt sore under his breastbone. Even Lucas talked approvingly in terms of *we*.

"With a scythe, son." *Better not call* me *son!* Tyler growled silently. "Someday there'll be machines to do it, but that's the only way we got now."

"And after that?" Tyler wondered aloud.

Perhaps Mr. Snepp could read minds, Tyler reflected, because he avoided the *s* word when he replied. "We'll let it dry for several days, Tyler, till all the leafy parts wither and fall off. Then we'll make bundles of the dried stalks, load them into the wagon, and I'll take 'em over to St. Joe to market."

Mr. Snepp wasn't one to put things off even an hour and got his scythe out of the wagon. Then he and Isaac, being tallest, took turns cutting the hemp stalks. Tyler and Lucas went along behind and carefully laid the stalks in rows to dry in the sun. Sooner ran back and forth checking on everyone, as if he'd appointed himself the crew boss. Afterward Mr. Snepp got ready to head home again, where his own hemp crop was drying while Oat minded the younger children.

"My, I'll certainly be glad when we're all living under the same roof," Elway told Lucas with a sigh. Tyler glanced across the rows of hemp and hardened his spirit against such a day. At the last minute, surely Mama would change her mind.

* * *

Tyler woke before either Lucas or Isaac had stirred. There was no familiar slurp-slurp from the little pine bed against the far wall because after Isaac came to stay, Rosa Lee always slept downstairs.

Dust motes danced cheerfully in the shafts of sunlight that came through the high east window, yet Tyler felt sorrow weigh him down in spite of the early hour. *Why should that be,* he asked himself, when he hadn't had time yet to rub the nighttime sand out of his eyes?

He raised himself on one elbow. Why, there were actually three boys still asleep in the loft this morning! Cousin Clayton was curled up on a pallet in the very spot where Rosa Lee's bed used to be. The sight of Clayton suddenly brought the day sharply into focus.

Mama's wedding day had arrived.

The dull ache in Tyler's chest turned to fierce pain. Oh, he'd been so sure something would happen to bring her to her senses! He didn't actually wish harm to come to Mr. Snepp, yet over the past weeks he'd imagined Elway falling out of the haymow over there at his place . . . his mules bolting with the wagon so he broke a leg . . . him catching some kind of sickness that didn't actually kill him but kept him laid up at home for a long time. Given the chance to collect her wits, Mama would surely realize she didn't need Mr. Snepp, that his brood of sons could manage on their own after all.

Below, Tyler heard his mother rattling the grate and making soft woman-talk with Rosa Lee. Aunt Margaret and Uncle Matt, who'd come to Sweet Creek with Clayton two days ago, still must be asleep in the back room. Quickly, Tyler pulled on his clothes and hurried downstairs. He'd try one final time to talk sense into Mama and silently rehearsed what he planned to say.

He'd pledge to stay by her side forever.

He'd agree to plant any kind of crazy crop she wanted—more hemp, if that was her heart's desire.

He'd promise never to drink spirits, like Papa did.

"Mama, there's something I've got to talk to you about," Tyler announced when he got downstairs. He combed his hair hastily with his fingers. He didn't bother to splash water on his face or scrub his hands in the washbowl she set out for him. It was important to say what he had to say while everyone else—except Rosa Lee—was still asleep.

"Why, Tyler, I'm glad you do," Mama declared. Her voice was warm, and he saw a mild, pleased expression in her blue eyes. "There's been something I've wanted to talk to you about, too, son. While Rosa Lee stirs up some mush, why don't we step out on the porch."

"You can talk in front of me!" Rosa Lee exclaimed. "I won't tell anybody—not even if Aunt Margaret begs me and says she'll whack me if I don't!"

Mama kissed the top of Rosa Lee's head. "Of course you wouldn't, dear. But this is a special day, and Ty and I need a moment to ourselves, just like you and I had time together last night before we went to sleep, remember?"

Mama sat down on the top step of the porch. Tyler was determined to stand up to say what was on his mind, but finally he hunkered down beside her. One thing was for sure: If a person had ordered up a perfect day for a wedding, this was it. Everything was fresh and alive—the smell in the air, the sound of the birds, the distant murmur of the creek under the bridge. In the garden, the squash were bright gold; the pole beans were still bearing; the onion tops stuck out of the black soil as shiny and sharp as swords.

Mama placed her hand on his knee. Tyler thought she

merely meant to give him a pat, but she left it there, a cozy hat over his kneecap. "I know this has been hard for you, Ty," she began. "Seeing your mama take another man's name can't be an easy thing." It was clear she'd been thinking about what she wanted to say, too.

"Lucas and Rosa Lee seem to have taken to the idea better, but I understand why you can't. Not yet, at any rate. You are your papa's firstborn son. You're the one who went off to search for him. It means you're special, Ty."

Tyler didn't want to be told he was special. It might soften his heart against what would happen later today. "It just don't seem right," he insisted. "Me and Lucas committed Papa's spirit right up there on the hill. We're all together now, so—"

"And I'm most grateful for that," Mama broke in. "I'm glad Isaac brought Papa's farewell letter to us, that the pretty blue aggie came back to you, Ty. But Papa's been gone for almost five years. Now we know he's gone forever. We can treasure his memory, but it's time for all of us to get on with the business of living."

"We were doin' fine, Mama! Why does the business of living mean you got to marry Mr. Snepp?" Tyler demanded.

"Elway and I have something in common," Mama explained. "He lost a wife. I lost a husband. Between us, we've got a flock of children to raise—goodness, there are ten of you in all!—and it makes fine, common sense for us to do it together. Little Henry is barely three. He needs a mother. And it will be good for Rosa Lee to have a father."

"Yes, it will!" Rosa Lee called from the other side of the door. "But I won't tell Aunt Margaret, not even if she begs me to!" The pest. She'd been listening to every word.

Tyler moved aside so Mama had to lift her hand from his knee. He'd never believed he was like Papa. Certainly not in the same way Lucas and Rosa Lee were, with their black, gypsy eyes and tousled midnight-colored hair. Just the same, there must be something of Papa inside him, because deep down Tyler felt Black Jack Bohannon's iron will stiffen his backbone. No way could he accept Elway Snepp as a substitute for Papa. No way would he ever bend on the matter.

"I want you to wish us well, Ty," Mama finished. There was a beseeching note in her voice. "It won't be easy, putting two families together, but Elway and I aim to do our best. We need everybody's help, son."

Suddenly, Tyler didn't feel like her son. They were strangers to one another. The dreams they dreamed were wildly different: He wanted to keep all the Bohannons together; she'd set herself to become a mother to the Snepp children.

Tyler rose abruptly from his place on the step. "I think Rosa Lee's got the mush ready," he said curtly. He knew he'd never be able to say, *I wish you well*. Never! Those four words stuck in his throat and refused to march past his teeth.

Mama and Aunt Margaret had baked pies and cookies for two days. Everyone, Isaac included, had taken their baths the evening before. Mama had already trimmed Lucas's and Tyler's hair. Now all that needed to be done was to dress, then await the arrival of the Snepp clan.

Tyler's new shirt made his neck itch. He scratched and toyed with the wicked hope that misfortune would befall the whole lot of Snepps on their journey to Sweet

Creek. Alas, when their wagon clattered across the bridge at noon, they were all alive and accounted for. The Reverend Wilbur Tucker rode on the wagon bench beside Mr. Snepp, and the Snepp boys were scrubbed and shining—Oat the shiniest one of all. Elway wore his black funeral suit, but he'd plucked a yellow rose from the roadside and had tucked it in his buttonhole.

Tyler supposed a wedding ceremony took a long time. Everyone would have to stand under the oak tree in the yard for hours, getting sweatier and itchier in their dress-up clothes. The Reverend Tucker clearly was an old hand at marrying as well as burying, however, because he conducted the service speedily. Tyler tried hard not to hear any of the words. There was one part, though, when Reverend Tucker posed a question to the gathering that shocked him to attention.

"Are there any among you today who know why this couple should not be joined together in holy matrimony? Speak now, or forever hold your peace."

Speak now! . . . The order came like a command from on high. Tyler opened his mouth. He saw Mama flash him a wary glance.

My mama's name is Ellen Bohannon! Tyler longed to cry out. *She married Papa for life—his life and hers, too! Papa said he wanted to meet us all again in the Great Beyond—but he didn't mean for Elway Snepp to tag along!*

But he held his tongue and bowed his head. He closed his eyes when Reverend Tucker announced, "I now pronounce you man and wife." *Man and wife.* The deed was done. Tyler felt a knife go through his breastbone and snip his heartstrings into useless pieces.

No one else suffered any pain, though. Nossir, you'd swear Lucas and Rosa Lee had ordered up Mr. Snepp special right out of a catalog. Tyler could understand how it was with Rosa Lee: she'd been less than a year old when Papa went off to war. To her, it probably seemed fine and dandy that today she'd become the daughter Mr. Snepp never had. *But Lucas?* There was something traitorous about how swiftly he'd accepted Papa was gone for good. He'd shrugged off the past like it was an old coat that didn't fit anymore.

After the ceremony, the menfolk moved the kitchen table out under the oak tree, and Mama and Aunt Margaret heaped it with food—golden fried chicken, snowy mountains of mashed potatoes, green beans seasoned with dill weed, scarlet pickled beets—then straightaway folks started to eat like it was the happiest day ever. Pies and cakes were added later, and lemonade was poured from a fancy pitcher Aunt Margaret had fetched from her place down in New Hope. Afterward Uncle Matt and Elway Snepp gabbed like long-lost friends. Reverend Tucker stretched out under the oak tree and took a nap. Cousin Clayton and Oat put their heads together as if they actually had something in common. Tyler was sure they didn't.

It was enough to make any sensible person throw up.

Tyler picked at his food, had no appetite even for cake or lemonade, and finally took refuge in the weeds behind the cow shed. Even foxy Sooner stayed behind, preferring the excitement of company and the chance to gobble up tasty morsels dropped by the younger Snepps. When Isaac finally followed him, Tyler turned his face aside as if he preferred solitude and company was unwelcome.

"My, he be a good man, your mama's Mr. Snepp," Isaac observed, patting his own full belly.

Mama's Mr. Snepp. Well, that's what he was now. After today, the two of them belonged to each other. Tyler sighed.

"I been thinkin'," Isaac said, settling himself in the weeds. He was togged out as fine as anyone else at the wedding. Since he was a good-sized boy, Mama had given him one of Papa's old shirts to wear, a white one with a ruffle on the front, and his trousers were freshly cleaned and mended.

"What about?" Tyler muttered. It was plain Isaac hadn't gotten the hint that company wasn't welcome.

"About movin' on after we take that hemp crop to St. Joe. Yessir, that's what I been thinkin', Ty."

"Why? Ain't we treated you right enough?" Of course, Tyler knew exactly what had put such an idea into Isaac's head. He was holding a grudge, that's why. "It's on account of what I almost said, ain't it? That business about you bein' uppity and all?"

"Naw! I almost forgot that, Ty." The way Isaac said it almost made Tyler believe he was telling the truth.

"How come, then?"

Isaac fixed his glance in the distance. "Ain't you ever had the feeling they's times for a person to stay and times for a person to go?"

Times to stay . . . times to go. Tyler let the words sink in. They sounded a lot like what had been going through his own mind lately.

"See, that's how it be when I was down there in New Orleans," Isaac explained. "You know, when that man gave me the letter and that blue aggie? Why, I knew right then it was time for me to light out."

"Shoot, I ain't never had such feelings," Tyler lied. He stared across Patches's sagging back to where the dogwoods lined the creek. Sounds of laughter from the table under the oak tree floated over the top of the cow shed and fell like misty rain on his spirits. "So where you aim to go?" he asked dully.

"Down to New Hope with your uncle Matt and cousin Clayton. Remember, Clayton said I could. He tol' me that black man who lives back of your uncle Matt's livery stable—name's Henry, ain't it?—he'd be glad to have my company for a spell."

"New Hope is way to the south," Tyler pointed out. He paused. "Why don't we head west?"

"*We?* Who this *we* you talkin' about, Ty?" Isaac guffawed. "You got a itty-bitty pig in your pocket, or what?" He slapped his knee lightly, delighted with his little joke.

"Nowadays people of all ages are headed west. I just read about it in the newspaper. That's why Mr. Snepp—Elway, I mean—that's why Elway's so keen on raising hemp. To make rope and cordage and canvas, so all those folks going that way will be well supplied."

"West," Isaac murmured skeptically. "Umm, Isaac Peerce don't know nothin' 'bout the West."

Even before school let out for the year, Tyler hadn't been able to take his eyes off the map tacked on the wall in Mr. Blackburn's class. If a person had a mind to, he could leave Missouri, cross right over into Kansas, then head overland for the Rocky Mountains. Mr. Blackburn said Indians called them the Shining Mountains because their tops were so tall, the snow never melted even in the middle of the summer.

Or a person could go down to St. Joe, head up the Missouri River on a keelboat, then go all the way to Fort Benton out there in Montana Territory. The word *territory* made it sound wilder than an ordinary place. If the time had come for a person to leave home, why not hit for the wildest place on the map?

"I don't know anything about it, either," Tyler admitted. "Maybe we could find out together." Isaac turned slowly and stared into Tyler's eyes. Tyler stared back.

"Mr. Sn—Elway—he'll be taking that hemp crop to market in a few days. You and me could go with him, Isaac."

Tyler couldn't believe what he'd just said.

He was ready to leave Sweet Creek. . . .

Chapter Sixteen

AFTER THE WEDDING, Elway took his gaggle of boys home while the hemp crop finished drying on the hillside. During his absence, Mama started to pack her pots and pans and quilts.

"Elway says everything should be ready to load into his wagon the minute he comes back from St. Joseph, so's we can move straight over to his place," she said, smiling. "Elway says it surely will be a pleasure for all of us to commence our lives together."

Tyler listened. No anger warmed his blood. For a change, his untethered heart rested quietly in his chest. *Elway says; Elway says.* It was fitting that it would always be *Elway says* now; after all, they were man and wife. With Elway gone for a few days, however, Tyler realized there'd never be a better time to tell Mama what he'd decided to do.

"Mama, I won't be movin' up the creek with you," he announced. She stared at him, astonished, then a frown creased her brow.

"Not moving, Ty? Whatever do you mean, son? That you aim to stay all alone here at Sweet Creek? Or do you plan to have Lucas stay behind with you?" She wagged her head disapprovingly. "Umm—I reckon we'd best discuss this with Elway!" She set her mouth in a no-nonsense way that reminded Tyler of his argument with her about where Isaac would eat and sleep. She'd let him win that one; this one might not be so easy.

"No, ma'am, I don't aim to stay here alone," Tyler said. "Don't mean to have Lucas stay with me, either." Mama's frown deepened. She plucked nervously at her apron, then gathered up a stack of dishes to pack in a barrel.

"The thing is, Mama, there's a time to stay and a time to go," Tyler explained, quoting Isaac as if he were an authority equal to Mr. Blackburn. "What I aim to do is go to St. Joe with Elway."

Mama sighed with relief, fanning her cheek as if he'd given her a good scare. "Gracious, why didn't you say so right out! I know he'll be glad to have your company, son. If the two of you can spend time alone together, perhaps you can come to a meeting of your minds."

"Me and Elway won't exactly be alone, Mama. Isaac's goin' along with us," Tyler said. He hesitated. She'd just said *say so right out;* all right, he would. "The other thing is, neither me or Isaac are coming back to Sweet Creek."

"Not coming back?" Mama whispered those three words in a child's faint afraid-of-the-dark voice. Tyler regretted the look that crept into her eyes, especially since he remembered how happy she'd been only a few days ago as she stood under the oak tree out in the yard and became Mrs. Elway Snepp.

Tyler moved quickly to take the stack of dishes from her before she dropped them. "Mama, Isaac and me have decided to go out to the territories to test our luck," he explained. "There was an article in the McMinnville newspaper—the very one with the news about Papa that you cut out and put in your Bible—that said lots of folks are goin' out there, even young ones like Isaac and me. There's work and land to be had, the article said, and we crave to try our hand like everyone else."

Mama smoothed her cheek with trembly fingertips. "We'll have to ask Elway what he thinks," she insisted, as if nothing had been decided yet.

"No, Mama, we won't." Tyler was surprised at the steadfastness of his reply. "I don't think Elway craves to tell me what to do—or *not* to do—any more'n I want him to." Elway hadn't called him son, had he? Hadn't leaned on him in any way, had he? Nossir. In fact, right from the get-go, Elway had treated him almost like— well, almost like a man.

As Tyler suspected, Mama was determined to have her way this time. "Son, we will indeed discuss it with Elway! Just as soon as he comes back from up yonder." Tyler shrugged. So be it. But he wasn't old and crippled like Patches; now that he'd made his decision, neither Mama nor Elway could build a fence high enough to pen him in.

Meantime, there was someone else who had to be told. Telling him wouldn't be any easier than telling Mama, but it might as well be done now, too.

Tyler waited until he and Lucas went up the hillside to check the hemp. The stalks were dry and brittle; it was time to gather them up and tie them in bundles that could be loaded in Elway's wagon for the trip to St. Joe. Sooner occupied himself with dashing between the rows to feast on the mice that were flushed from under the stalks. Tyler decided not to beat around the bush. He'd tell Lucas in the plainest words he could find.

"Lucas, I'm going away again," he said.

"Away? Away where?"

"I'm goin' to ride down to St. Joe with Elway."

"Say now, that sounds like fun, Ty! Can I go along?"

There really wasn't any reason why he couldn't, Tyler realized. "Why, that'd be a good idea, Lucas. Isaac's goin', too. But we won't be coming back from St. Joe with you."

Lucas turned and wore the same stunned expression of dismay that Mama had. "Won't be coming back?" he echoed, straightening up from his bundling job. "But there's no cause for you to go away again, Ty! There ain't no need to go lookin' for Papa again. We already know what happened to him. And didn't you hear what Elway said? Someday, you and me can farm this place together. Besides, you're the one who told me we should always remember we're brothers—"

Quickly, Tyler quoted Isaac again, about going and staying. "I think he's got a point, Lucas. There *is* a time to go and a time to stay. For Isaac and me, it's time to go find out what's out there in the territories. But that doesn't mean you and me aren't still brothers, Lucas."

Lucas dropped his arms to his sides. He fastened his glance on Sooner as the dog darted back and forth. "I s'pose you aim to take him with you," he murmured, sinking to his knees and calling Sooner to his side. He looped both arms around the dog's neck. Tyler watched as his brother buried his face in Sooner's thick red ruff.

"You said Sooner was goin' to be a family dog," Lucas reminded Tyler, his words muffled in Sooner's thick fur. "You said he'd belong to you and me together, not just one of us." He stuck his face even deeper into the dog's neck. "You set on takin' him because of what I did in the cow shed that day?"

"Why, shoot, Lucas, I almost totally forgot about that!" Tyler exclaimed. It was true; he had. But if that were so, why couldn't he leave Sooner behind?

"It's on account of Bigger that I want to take him with me," he admitted. Bigger and Sooner; each of them belonged to precious parts of his past—Bigger because of his loyalty on that long trip to Texas, Sooner because he was Bigger's only son. Suddenly, Tyler knew something else: There *was* something he intended to leave behind with Lucas.

When his brother turned Sooner loose and rose to his feet, Tyler saw Lucas blink a silver tear from the corner of his eye. "After you get moved up to Elway's big house, Lucas, I'll bet you can talk him into getting you a new dog," he soothed. "Check with Uncle Matt; maybe his little Daisy hound has got a new batch of pups by now. Between now and then, there's something I aim to leave with you—"

Lucas whisked the telltale water off his cheek, pretending it was a fly. Tyler reached into his pocket and took out Papa's blue aggie. "Hold out your hand, Lucas." When he did, Tyler dropped the pale marble into his brother's cupped palm.

"It was the nicest thing Papa ever gave me, Lucas. That's the reason I want you to have it now. For all time—no matter what happens in life—it'll remind you of Papa . . . of me . . . and being such a funny blue color that looks like one of Sooner's eyes, it'll remind you of him, too. Long as you got that aggie, Lucas, you'll have a little piece of each one of us."

Lucas stared into his palm and sucked in his breath. "I promise I'll take good care of it, Ty." He folded his fingers around the marble and held it fast. "Will you write back and tell me what the territories are like, Ty?"

"You bet I will," Ty promised. He imagined the letters he'd send home, letters Lucas would treasure as he himself treasured Papa's once upon a time. Lucas could

take those letters to Mr. Blackburn's class to read aloud—
let that tub of lard, Joshua Simons, turn green as a pea!

Lucas slipped the aggie into his pocket. "You still
willin' to let me ride to St. Joe with you, Ty?" he asked
hopefully.

Tyler looped an arm around his brother's shoulder,
remembering the way they'd hung on to each other when
they went over to the Snepps' to strike a deal for Patches.
"Surely am, Lucas. Elway will be glad to have your company on the way back."

When Lucas announced at the supper table what he
intended to do, Rosa Lee made it plain she didn't intend
to be left behind. "If Lucas goes, I'm going, too!" she
vowed. If Elway Snepp figured he'd gotten a daughter
who'd take no for an answer very often, he'd better think
again, Tyler mused. He glanced swiftly at Mama. Her
lips were pulled tight, as if to say, *We'll just see what
Elway says about all this!*

When Elway arrived two days later, Rosa Lee wasted
no time letting him know he'd have four passengers
going down to St. Joe but the number would shrink to
two for the trip home. Elway laid a freckled hand on
Rosa Lee's head. "But I take it my dear little missy will be
one of those who come back," he said, as unperturbed as
if she were telling tales. He gave her a fond look, still surprised to have acquired a girl child. Even when Rosa Lee
was a handful, Tyler knew Elway Snepp would always
love her.

"Let me remind you all that no decision has been
made about anyone but Elway going to St. Joe," Mama
declared, and braced her hands on her hips. "Lucas and
Isaac, you boys load our portion of hemp into Elway's

wagon. Rosa Lee, you go down and get the eggs. Tyler and Elway and I need time for a private conversation."

"Private?" Rosa Lee objected. "But I won't tell anyone, not if they call me names or kick me or pull my hair!"

"Rosie, my Rosie—do as your mama says," Elway soothed, and surprisingly (without stamping her feet!) Rosa Lee did as she was bid.

Mama sat at the table, her face grim, her hands locked in front of her. Elway laid his hat on the table and sat down, too. Papa's old chair near the window was empty; Tyler eased himself into it. For the first time, it seemed to fit.

"Tyler says he's not goin' to move with us," Mama said tersely. Elway turned, brows raised, a question in his pale eyes. He waited for Tyler to speak.

"Mr. Sn—Elway, I mean—Isaac and me have decided we want to light out for the territories. Isaac's ready to move on—and I aim to go with him."

"Elway, tell him he can't do any such thing," Mama ordered. "He's way too young! He's only been hunting once in his life! There's no way he can—"

"Now, Ellen. Now, Ellen," Elway said patiently. "Remember, this is the boy who went searching for his papa more'n a year ago," he reminded her. "He made a long and lonesome journey *all by himself* way down to Texas and came safely home again."

Tyler saw tears spring to his mother's eyes. "But Elway— would you let Oat do such a thing as Tyler's fixing to do?"

Elway smiled. "Dear wife! Oat is his father's son— but your boy Tyler is *his* father's son. Black Jack Bohannon was a brave man who rode off to take a stand for what he believed. Tyler doesn't aim to go off to war;

he wants to go exploring—yet his convictions spring from the same place in the heart that his papa's did."

The words hung in the air above the table. Tyler was even more stunned than Mama. *Elway understood!* Pale, freckled, chipmunk-cheeked Elway Snepp knew him better than his own mother did!

"Elway! You mean you're not going to tell Tyler that he can't—" Mama protested.

Elway covered Mama's hands with his large pale ones before he interrupted her. "No, my dear, I'm not. Some folks aren't meant for safe pastures. Maybe Tyler is one of 'em, just like his papa before him."

After the wagon was loaded and while Mama packed food for the trip, Tyler went alone to the top of the hill where Papa's spirit had been committed. Autumn had colored the countryside with red and gold, and on a distant slope he could make out the three apple trees, already leafless, that stood guard over Bigger's grave.

Isaac's song came back to him: *You may bury me in the East, You may bury me in the West . . .* The West. "You'd understand what I'm doing, Papa," Tyler murmured. "And you know what? Elway Snepp does, too."

Tyler paid a farewell call on Patches. During the summer, the old gaffer had cultivated the hemp crop in fine fashion. Now, Tyler laid his hand fondly over the patch that caused Mama to give him his name.

"If it hadn't been for you calling for help when those scalawags showed up, we might've been cleaned out," Tyler told him. Patches blinked his silver lashes as if he were shy about accepting compliments.

"When I'm traveling down to St. Joe, I'm going to make Elway promise you can live out your days in peace and comfort," Tyler said. "Lucas can give you chores to do from time to time. You won't be left to stand in back of the barn till you topple over dead."

After everyone had gotten in the wagon, Tyler lingered alone in the kitchen and cast a final glance around the cabin where he'd been born. Up the ladder toward the sleeping loft . . . through the small window beneath which Papa used to sit . . . at the stove where Mama had roasted the haunch of venison. No matter where he went, he'd carry such memories with him.

Then he retrieved the Hawken from its place behind the door of Mama's bedroom, turned on his heel, and strode onto the porch. As he headed toward the wagon, Tyler caught a glimpse of his short, stocky shadow resolutely keeping pace beside him. It's on account of the angle of the sun that it seems so short, he told himself wryly.

Settling the Hawken in the crook of his arm, Tyler prepared to hoist himself into the wagon, to take his place beside Isaac. "Best leave the Hawken behind with your mama, seeing she'll be alone till I get back tomorrow," Elway advised gently.

Tyler took a swift step backward. "I figured me and Isaac would be needin' it where we're going," he replied tersely. An hour ago Elway had seemed almost like a friend. How could he turn so suddenly into an enemy?

Elway reached under the wagon bench and drew out his gleaming blue-barreled Winchester. "Take this with you, son. The Hawken will do us fine, but I hear there's bear and cougar and wolf and such critters out where you're headed." He'd never used the *s* word before; it sounded proper now.

Tyler passed the Hawken to Elway and took the Winchester in return. He swallowed hard. "Why, thanks." Then he turned one last time to Mama.

Four words were stuck in his throat, words that finally demanded to be said. "Mama—I'd like to—I wish you well," he blurted. They were out before he could think twice. He said them again. "You and Elway both—I wish you well."

Tears leaped to his mother's eyes again, but this time they weren't bitter ones. She took the Hawken, then gave him a long farewell hug.

Tyler climbed into the wagon beside Isaac. Lucas and Rosa Lee rode proudly on the wagon bench beside their new stepfather. Sooner followed, but in no time was distracted by a rabbit and darted away on another futile chase.

The wheels of Elway's wagon echoed hollowly across the bridge over Sweet Creek. Behind him, Tyler knew that Mama, the snug cabin, the sturdy cow shed, the root cellar that had been a prison for two scalawags, all receded steadily into the distance. He settled the Winchester comfortably across his knees.

The strings that held his heart in place felt as if they'd been newly mended, and he exchanged a smile with Isaac. "Tell me some more about them names you found on Mr. Blackburn's map," Isaac suggested.

"Oh, there's a flock of 'em," Tyler said. "Three Forks and the Wind River Range and Green River—so many I can hardly remember 'em all." He told Isaac what Mr. Blackburn said about the twelve-year-old Shoshone girl named Grass Maiden who'd been stolen from her tribe at the convergence of Three Rivers, then renamed Sacagawea by her captors. How Jedediah Smith stumbled down the slopes of the Wind River Range on a snowy moonlit night in 1824, the wind so fierce it froze his eyelids shut. How on the banks of the Green River in

1835, a young missionary named Marcus Whitman removed an arrowhead from the hip of Jim Bridger.

Tyler whistled for Sooner. "*Soooo*ner! C'mon, boy!" he called. "We're heading west!"

The red dog flew down from the apple trees that guarded Bigger's grave, the bib on his chest as fresh and white as if it had been washed this morning. Tyler looked down; Sooner looked up, cheerfully waving his plumy, fox-colored tail. His brown eye gleamed with eagerness for fresh adventure; the blue one reflected coolly on ancient tales passed down to him from his Highland ancestors.

Tyler Bohannon smiled. He squared his shoulders. He didn't look back.

After . . .

Heading westward was nothing new to Americans. From the moment the nation was colonized, its citizens had turned their eyes ever toward the West. In the beginning, the protective forest walls of New York State, of Pennsylvania, of Kentucky, were a barrier that invited curiosity. "What lies beyond them?" men and women asked themselves. The impulse to find out was irresistible.

Long before the Civil War commenced in April 1861, men such as Davy Crockett and Daniel Boone went west to discover what lay in the land where the sun set. Then, with the signing by Abraham Lincoln of the Homestead Act in 1862, designed specifically to open the West for settlement as soon as the War Between the States was over, the flow of emigration beyond the Mississippi increased dramatically.

Americans fervently believed that out west not only would they find cheaper land and achieve a certain kind of independence, but they could also wipe away the injuries of war. Not all Civil War wounds were suffered on famous battlefields such as Bull Run or Shiloh, or less famous ones like Stones River or Pea Ridge. The war broke families apart, and it was in the West that new lives could be forged.

After the war, something else happened that had never been possible before: Black folk could choose lives for themselves. They no longer had to endure fates that were chosen for them by white masters. The Freedmen's Aid Societies of various churches and the American Missionary Society were among charitable organizations that helped black men and women adjust to the challenges of freedom.

For the first time, black and white folk could head west as equals, and sometimes they did exactly that. Perhaps it was as the poet Carl Sandburg later wrote:

> *Man is born with rainbows in his heart*
> *and you'll never read him unless you consider*
> *rainbows.*